CORNISH RHAPSODY

In order to forget the handsome but unreliable Dr Edgar Thorn, Nurse Bridget Smythe goes to Cornwall to look after Gay Sutcliffe, a famous writer suffering from rheumatoid arthritis. On the train she meets Alan Thane, a neighbouring farmer, and then later, Julian Clare, Miss Sutcliffe's adopted nephew, and the irascible GP, Dr Forbes. Bridget finds Gay charming, but she soon senses that all is not well in the household. Why are Julian and Dr Forbes so averse to her suggestions that a more advanced treatment be tried on the patient? And what was a used hypodermic needle doing lying in an ashtray, hours after Gay's daily injection?

CORNISH RHAPSODY

URSULA BLOOM
as Sheila Burns

A Lythway Book

CHIVERS PRESS
BATH

First published in Great Britain 1972
by
Robert Hale & Company
This Large Print edition published by
Chivers Press
by arrangement with the author
1984

ISBN 0 85046 978 3

British Library Cataloguing in Publication Data

Burns, Sheila
   Cornish rhapsody.—Large print ed.
   —(A Lythway book)
   Rn: Ursula Bloom   I. Title
   823'.912[F]   PR6003.L58

   ISBN 0–85046–978–3

CORNISH RHAPSODY

CHAPTER ONE

Bridget Smythe was dressing for the hospital ball, the great occasion of the year, for which everyone tried to beg, borrow or steal an exciting dress—the night of nights. She wanted to look her best, and that the frock on which all her savings had gone, would look as lovely as it had done in the shop; but of course that never happened. One could not explain it, or why it changed, but change it did.

Tonight was special for her.

Bridget supposed that she had been in love with Edgar Thorn for a whole year now, and although she kept telling herself that it was reaching the point when he simply *must* say something, he had never said it yet. She had quivered on the edge of longing—for him.

'I've something special to ask you tonight,' he had said only this morning, but he had got as far as that before. He was always talking of 'something special' that he wanted to ask her, something very extra special, but it had never yet come.

'It must be tonight,' she told herself.

She was a sensitive, warm-hearted girl, the kind who trusted people, and she believed in Edgar Thorn. She knew, of course, that the hospital had given him the pet name of the

1

'Hospital Jilt', for he was attractive and it was said that he had broken more hearts than he had ever mended; his job in the hospital was cardiac. In the theatre Bridget had been warned against him, but somehow his charm had obliterated all that; she had always told herself that she could never let any man break her heart, but in life these things happen.

'Have I been a fool about Edgar?' she asked herself, but felt that that was ridiculous. He was bound to marry somebody some day. Why could it not be herself?

*   *   *

Bridget came here to train when she was old enough. Her father, a doctor working in the poorer part of Grimsby, had worked himself to death there, fighting cancer, sickness and poverty until he could take no more.

'One day you will follow in my steps, darling,' he had said to her, a memory which now was fading with time. 'But never drive yourself too hard, for that does not help you, or anybody else, I warn you of that.'

She had not been sufficiently clever to follow in his steps, and when she peeped inside the books he had left behind him, she wondered how he had done it. But she had promised to follow him, and that was why she had started training as a nurse.

At the time she had been sure that she would never qualify, for the exams were so difficult, her memory bad, and she fluffed it twice, and was put back a whole six months for that.

'I'd never try again,' said Carrie Hinton, a naughty little girl who never tried too hard. She was the nightmare of the Sisters, constantly being reproved by Matron, ignored by doctors, but the darling of the medical students.

Now, at last, Bridget had qualified. She had sat for the finals with the worst cold of her life. Never for a moment did she think that she would pass, then she saw Sir Charles Rowley on the board, and he was sorry for her. 'With that cold you ought to be in bed, not here; you'll have pneumonia next week,' he prophesied. She admitted that she had to get through this time, or die in the attempt, and she almost thought that death would be welcome. He was kind, comforting, and reassuring, and to her dying day she would believe that she owed her triumph to him.

When the moment came when the names of the successful candidates would be pinned up on the board in the main hall, Bridget had not dared to go down to have a look. Too much depended on it. She sent little Freda Adams instead. She was, of course, quite convinced that she had failed; it had been those dreadful questions which had come up about rheumatoid arthritis, never her strongest point. Thinking of

3

it later, she was sure that all the answers that she had given must have been wrong.

Freda returned from the main hall and she was enchanted with glee. Bridget had got through! How, nobody knew, but she had done it. Surely there must be some awful mistake? the girl thought, but she had the courage to avail herself of the 'awful mistake', and as the board said that she had qualified, she accepted it as being just that! She went wild with excitement, and was thrilled to the marrow.

She was approaching the moment when she made up her mind as to what she would do next. The choice lay between signing on for two years, or breaking away to pastures new, and bigger chances.

*   *   *

As she slipped into the sea-green dress which had cost every penny that she had, she was trying to make up her mind as to the future. She thought of the things other nurses had done, where they had gone and the possibilities offered to them. After all, one must think of oneself a little. Nursing is hard work, it is also monotonous. She thought of the flying nurses, but this had always alarmed her, and although they said one became accustomed, given time, that time must be almost unendurable! A nurse on the big liners got bored, she was told, and,

4

anyway, why she had contemplated it she could not think, for she herself was a bad sailor. Her only effort so far had been when staying with an aunt in Dover, and they had gone over to Calais for an afternoon. The sea was so rough that she never went ashore in France, because she felt so ill, and the prospect of the return journey dismayed her to despair.

There seemed to be something against all the exciting jobs, when you started to think about them, but the idea of staying on for two years in hospital seemed deadly dull. She wanted adventure, and she wanted it badly.

Sister Tutor had advised her to do nothing in a hurry. She was a charming woman, and a good adviser, also fond of the girls whom she had trained. She had said, 'And now, don't dash off and marry one of the good-looking doctors just because he *is* good-looking, and for the thrill of the moment, for it doesn't pay. Stay in a set job for a few months, then see something of the world, but learn more first. That *is* wise.'

Sister had caught her with Edgar Thorn, talking one night outside the Titon ward, and perhaps she had noticed something. Other girls said she had the eyes of a hawk. Edgar had a bad name, and this was not really entirely his fault. Every good-looking medico who comes into a hospital falls under suspicion from the powers-that-be, and even the Warder (whose job it was to mind the students) raised his eyes to heaven

5

about Edgar.

The man could not help being tall and svelte, with charming eyes and a merry laugh. He knew that he was a winner. Only yesterday morning, when Bridget had been worried to death because the notices had not yet come through, Sister Tutor had smiled and said, 'If you do qualify (and a little bird tells me you have), forget Dr. Thorn, for he is the kind who never marry'.

That had hurt.

Now, all she knew was that the day was beautiful. She had come into the sunlit courtyard for a breath of fresh air; Edgar had passed by, and he had said, 'You and I have got to have a long talk, Bridget, now that you've got there. There is quite a lot for us to settle up, and I've waited too long.' He had tweaked her arm.

'I am the happiest girl in the world' was what she had told herself then.

The dress was a heavenly sea-green. She remembered that ages ago her mother had warned her that green was unlucky. Surely today people had more sense, and nobody listened to chit-chat of that kind? It was her colour, for it went admirably with her reddish hair. It had grown a shade lighter since she grew up, and now was almost a pure gold in some lights, but it had the glitter of red hair behind it all, which contradicted her temperament. She had been fortunate in dark brows and lashes. She liked the look of herself. 'And tonight has to be *the* night,' she told herself, 'for surely Edgar must say something at last?'

He was the sort of doctor the Sisters would never like, and she thought of that kind Sister who had been sweet about it, and had admitted that she hated seeing the girls getting their hearts torn to ribbons because they happened to get mixed up with some flirtatious young doctor who did not take life seriously.

She thought again of meeting him in the courtyard, and the thrill it had given her. He had said, 'I've got something to tell you, darling, something very precious.'

The words had made the rather sordid quadrangle (where all the doctors' cars were parked) look pleasant, almost a trysting place, almost beautiful. I've got it badly, she thought, and aloud to him, 'Tell me now?'

'I can't. We have been waiting for tonight, you know. Saved up for it, so to speak. Tonight will be *the* night of them all!'

She tied the light sash and thought with joy that it was almost time to hear what he had to say. 'This,' she told herself, 'is going to be *the* hour.' The green dress suited her; it had cost far far more than she could afford, of course, but this was such a very special occasion, and she felt that she must dress up for it.

She was wildly happy.

On the whole, Bridget would have said that she had had a hard life. Her charming father was a clever doctor who had died when she was a child, working himself to death. It had been a dreadful shock to her poor mother, left with practically nothing at all, and she had retired into a cheap little flat, and there she had kept the flag flying by doing odd jobs which offered themselves. In the end she had grown weary of eternal dressmaking, and that sort of thing, and had remarried when Bridget was twelve years old.

Bridget had not liked her stepfather. He had money, and everything was far more comfortable at home than it had been during the last few years. But he was a stern man, self-opinionated, and almost immediately her mother had found that she had made one of those ghastly mistakes. The marriage broke when Bridget was fifteen.

By that time she had grown older, and she had learnt that marriage could be difficult. She had also found that her mother was one of those simple women who go on making mistakes all their lives. She complained that life had been hard on her, that she had never had a chance, and had been worked to death, but most of it was her own fault.

She continually blamed Bridget's father, who should have insured his life, and of course had always meant to do so, but never had. To her horror, he had put nothing aside for his wife.

Possibly he had not thought that he would die

in the early thirties, and nobody likes having to save money when they themselves have so very little. Even when he had worn himself out with overwork, he vowed that he had only just begun to 'feel his way'. Mother had struggled for a time, then had married the first man who asked her, and who had the means to keep her. It was a tragedy that it had failed.

Bridget had gone off on a long visit to an aunt, and she never went back home. Her mother divorced her second husband, and married another doctor with a Harley Street address, which looked well. She had felt that this always brought a fortune with it. The man was a psychiatrist, one of those who think they know everything about everybody, though as far as Bridget could see, this particular man had not known so very much about her mother.

With the new marriage settled, and Mother living in a big flat off Portland Place, Bridget was established in her aunt's household. The aunt was kind, not too much in love with life, but good to the child, and she decided that a nurse's career was right for her, when she left the convent where she had been educated.

'Anyway it is a *good* career,' she said.

'I should have loved to be a doctor, but I am not clever enough,' the girl said.

'Then don't try it, for it is a long training and very depressing at times, they tell me.'

In the main, it was because she was so sure

that her father would have wished it, and she had a sentimental memory of this man who had worked himself to death, that she decided to become a nurse.

'I am sure Daddy would have wished it,' she said.

'Yes, of course he would, because men always want their children to follow their careers. You see, darling, your mother is a wee bit flighty, and he found that out before he died, and I think he wanted to get you away from it. Now, you be a nurse, and don't break your heart over some doctor, for that is not worth while. *Never* lose your heart, for that is sheer madness.'

The aunt, in the end got the girl into her father's old hospital to train, and this association did please her, and made her happier. It was harder going than even she had expected, just because she had been born with an indifferent memory. She could never learn off a string of names by heart, and then trot them out as required. She forgot them.

She worked hard. You have to in the medical field, if you are to get anywhere and do anything. It is no place for the lazybones, as Sister Tutor told her most impressively.

She had met Edgar Thorn.

Edgar was good-looking, buoyant and well pleased with himself, and what he was getting out of life. He had only just qualified when they first met. He was tall and slender, very handsome, one of those dark young men who allow their eyes to do the talking for them, and as Sister said, they talked too much! Unfortunately it was easy for Bridget to be guided by it. She was at the age when a girl is easily carried away; perchance in love with love, and ready to give up everything for it.

There was no doubt that the senior nursing staff summed him up and not entirely to his advantage, for Sisters learn the ways of doctors and are quick to condemn. Already Bridget grasped this. There was also no possibility whatsoever that the Warden (who was in charge of the medical students as they passed through the hospital) had not a fairly shattering opinion of this man. He had had to condemn him for too many scrapes, and, if anyone had asked him he would have insisted that Edgar Thorn was a very troublesome young man.

But beyond all that, the man had charm. He could whirl a girl off her feet, and knew this. Almost every one of the better-looking nurses had at some time or another passed through what was known as 'the Thorn phase', when they suffered from a crush on him. He admitted this, but said he could not avoid people falling in love with him. Bridget remembered an occasion when, as they came out of the operating theatre, he mentioned it. They had seen one of the most fascinating modern ops. done by one of the greatest men, and all of them had been on edge.

11

They had actually watched the life of the patient hanging on a string! But coming out, she had collided with Edgar Thorn, his dark eyes laughing.

'Of course everybody knows that I'm a bad lad,' he said, 'I am the Warden's panic, he has told me so, for I adore women. I was wondering if you could slip out to tea one day, and give me a treat?'

She knew that she had coloured; she had not yet outgrown that girlish trick of turning rosy when she was moved, or slightly shocked, or worried. The idea sent her dizzy with sheer joy, of course, because at that time she had set it far outside the realms of possibility.

She had not refused the invitation.

He had taken her out to the sort of tea about which one dreams, but is never likely to get in hospital, not even the paying patients. He had picked a pretty little teashop at the riverside, with the great, grey barges passing to and fro, and all the time the sound of the ships' sirens with that prolonged whining cry of theirs. It was a sweet little shop decorated in soft pink and green (unusual colours), and with comfortable chairs for a change.

'I must not fall in love with him' was what she kept telling herself, because he was not for her. Flirtations were everyday to a man like Edgar Thorn; he flirted and fooled, lost his heart and called it back again, and lived to flirt and fool yet another day.

She knew perfectly well what Matron and the doctors thought of him. She had been surprised when overhearing a talk the Warden had had about him, and very angry also, because she thought he was handsome, and a dear. He had deliberately indulged her; he was one of those lucky young men who are born with a silver spoon in their mouth, and he realised it. Now he had asked her out to tea, in a charming teashop.

The tea had been rewarding.

He told her of his home, his early life, devotion to a spoiling mother who was always pleasant to him. He had only scraped through, and knew that the senior surgeons thought nothing of him. That was not a worry, and as far as he was concerned the lack of affection was reciprocated. He talked of the ball, the annual affair, and she must be his partner.

She had not the heart to say 'no'.

Tea in a lime and peach restaurant had turned her head, and although the whole world would tell her that she was a little fool, she would not be guided. He was a charmer, so dark, so flattering, and so tender. Also, these things happen.

She had drawn out all her meagre savings to buy the very special green dress for the occasion. He had said that she must look her best, for he had something to say to her. She had even launched out into a new face cream which

13

cost the earth, and a shade of mascara which made all the difference in the world to her appearance.

She did her hair a new way, one advised by the hairdresser, and this too changed her appearance. She knew that she had a fresh, bright radiance which had come to her, and only prayed that she had the courage to go through with it. Edgar was a madly attractive man, and she loved him. 'This is the night' she told herself. She even forgot that tomorrow morning she had an appointment with Matron at 9.30. As you start for the most thrilling dance of the year, the worries of tomorrow recede, and become entirely matterless. You forget them.

'I can't be bothered' was her attitude now.

She knew perfectly well that Matron would ask her if she was prepared to come into the hospital, signing on for another two years with them. It was the usual request, and lots of girls fell into this trap because Matron impressed them with the fact that they should repay the hard labour which had gone into their training, and the fact that actual money had been spent on their instruction. They *should* pay back what had been done for them.

Blow tomorrow! she thought, a great deal can happen before tomorrow comes, and when it does come, let it look after itself. She put a last gloss on the soft, reddish hair. Why worry about tomorrow when it was still tonight? Why, indeed?

She was satisfied by the view in the little scrap of glass which was all one got in hospital, almost as if the authorities had told themselves that it would be utterly wrong to encourage a girl in vanity. She looked her best, and Edgar would be the first man in the world to notice the new dress, the gloss on her hair, and that tempting lipstick. The dress made her look taller, more svelte, and this *was* going to be the happiest night of her life. No more of those gruesome lectures! No more standing in the theatre till your feet seemed to swell like puddings, and weigh like lead. She was actually qualified and entering the future world. This was her night.

Approaching the ballroom, she could hear the sound of the band busying themselves with exotic introductory music. It was a sort of pot-pourri of modern tunes, but the sound of it was thrilling, and ahead lay adventure, perhaps the first real adventure in her life. She was in the mood to be dazzled by it: bright lights and shining floor, a few well-chosen decorations, and Matron in glowing plain clothes, which always took a bit of swallowing! One could not imagine Matron as a young woman in evening dress, but here she was. 'This is to be the most exciting night of all my life' she told herself.

'This is going to be real *fun*,' said little Patsy Moore, who had had trouble with Matron this very morning, and although Matron was an amiable woman and on the whole fair, she could lay down the law with agonizing firmness. 'I'm forgetting this morning. I may find myself kicked out within the month, but who cares a hoot about this now? This is the dance of the year, and I've got a new dress for it,' and to Bridget, 'You chose green? They say green is unlucky.'

That *had* to be the moment when she first saw Edgar Thorn!

The merry band had changed to vigorous dance music, the very latest piece, and there was Edgar with little Nelly Stein. Ten days ago Nelly was an unknown name in the hospital, none had heard of her. The Warden had produced her, she was his niece and he had got her here because she was a 'sweet piece'.

Nelly was far too pretty, her father a rich knight, who had made a fortune in something menial, like tin-tacks, and he was known as being something of a personality. And he was on the Board. This had made him an urgent influence in their world. Bridget had not really seen Nelly before, but now she had a full view of her dancing astoundingly well with Edgar. She was not tall, one of those bird-like little girls with laughing blue eyes, and a rose-flushed skin. She looked as if butter would not melt in her mouth, but then there are lots of girls who look like this but do not behave like it when it comes to a showdown. She distrusted Nelly on

16

sight, perhaps it was because she was with Edgar, and somehow she was ashamed of herself.

He had said that tonight he would have a lot to talk about to Bridget, and had conveyed the idea that this could easily be the time when they planned ahead. It might be idiotic, but already she had heard the distant pealing of wedding bells, seen herself in snow-white, and a veil on her head, and this *was* an inspiring thought.

Here he was dancing ecstatically with the prettiest girl in the room—she would have to accept this fact and have done with it—and she saw as they danced that their cheeks were together, and that Edgar was kissing her hair.

The sight was almost too much for her. Of course she knew that Edgar was flirtatious, even Sister Tutor had mentioned this to her, adding, 'I wanted to tell you, dear, because once I was young, and this can hurt badly.'

Sister Tutor was a pet. Privately Bridget had hated the warning at the time, but she had to admit that it came from a woman with a big heart. Sister Tutor had always been a darling, a woman who understood the troubles of youth, and was deeply sympathetic.

Bridget recoiled against the open doorway and watched the dancing. She had not felt that it would be like this; she had come here full of confidence that Edgar had something to say to her, and that he would say it. They had been as

17

good as engaged for weeks now, although he had never mentioned a ring, but that was natural. She, poor girl, was full of excuses for him. 'I love him so much,' she thought.

Little Jane Stevenson came up and stood beside her. She said, 'Your friend Edgar seems to have struck lucky, but he is the sort who always does. One of the conquering heroes in life, and every girl swears by him. I can see that he is having a magnificent time, and of course that girl Nelly's father *could* do a lot for him if it came to it. You bet Master Edgar knows where to lay his hand on the money!' and she started laughing.

That was when Bridget nearly broke down. In an agonized voice, a voice which was trying hard to hide the fact that she was desperate lest she began to cry, she said, 'Please don't!'

Mercifully, Jane had spotted the young student on whom she had had her eye for quite a time, and she pounced on him before somebody else made a pass in his direction. Jane never missed a chance, but then she was older than Bridget.

Helplessly Bridget went to a corner of the room and sat down on one of the gilt-painted chairs which come out for big occasions. The room looked lovely, with evergreens decorating it, pot palms and a whole bevy of glowing Cinerarias in violet, puce and cerise, on the platform where all the high-ups sat to watch proceedings. The room had been admirably done, for when it came to a dance the hospital gave a good one, and this was Joe Lewson's very special band, plaintively playing *Why did I lose that man, I loved him all the time?*

Unhappily the tune represented exactly what Bridget was feeling.

That was when Edgar waved to her. That, at least, was something; it meant that he had not completely forgotten that she lived in the same world as himself. She started to reassure herself that everything was going to be all right. Then he danced on again. He was talking hard to Nelly, and she was sure he would go on talking.

I must stop being a fool, she thought.

She danced with one student after another, little matterless dances, and all the time Edgar was spinning round with the new girl, and obviously enjoying himself very much. It was all the more maddening that she had been told that he was no good; warned by stern Sisters, cautiously warned by Sister Tutor. Then quite suddenly she sat down in a corner and he came and spoke to her.

'Darling, I don't know what you are thinking of me!' She wished that he was not so wildly attractive. The dark eyes danced, he had charm in a big way. 'I have to use power at court. Nelly's pa can move the earth for me, and my old man swears he will cut me off with a bob, which means that I have got to get somebody else to move the earth.'

'Of course.'

'Please forgive me, I can explain it all, and give me the first dance after the supper one, then I'll explain. We'll get married and live happily ever after. Trust your uncle!'

She should say 'no'. She ought to have the courage to send him about his business here and now, but the shocking thing was that she wanted him too much.

'All right,' she said, 'I'm on the second sitting, so it will mean that our dancing will be a bit abbreviated. I thought we had a lot to discuss?'

'We had, and we'll discuss it. You'll forgive me everything, my darling, when I tell you what has been happening, so don't worry yet.'

He flitted off again.

She danced with the casual students, the young doctors, then booked the supper dance with Frank Dene. He collected her before the dance actually began, a gracious, kindly, very earnest man. He would be thirty-five, she supposed. He had qualified early, though he had had two goes at 'midder' which had baulked him *pro tem*, to his fury. In the end he had got there, and she admired the courage of his persistence. It is of course easy to qualify if one has a good memory for names, but he could not get names into his head. He had got them one day, and the next had clean forgotten them.

They danced off together; it was her pet tune, and she saw Edgar still dancing with the divine Nelly, and apparently not one whit bored by her chatterbox activities.

Frank said, 'I must say your boyfriend is having a jolly good time with the Warden's guest. She's a pretty kid, but not one single ounce of sense in her. I should have said that she had power in high places, for her pa is on the Board, which always goes for something.'

'Yes,' and she hoped that her laugh sounded sincere.

'I'm afraid he is that sort of a lad! One of those who leave a trail of broken hearts behind them. All very nice for himself, he must get a lot of fun out of it, but it's very hard on the girls who suffer.'

'Yes, I know.' She prayed that she could laugh it off. It is very hard work laughing about something which you do not find in the least bit funny, but what else could she do? She did not think that Frank realized how near were her tears.

But she did not deceive him as well as she had hoped, for he took another look at her, then he said, 'Perhaps I know how you feel. Most of us suffer this way at some time in our lives, I know I did once, I thought I'd die of despair, but unhappily despair does not kill. What are you going to do next?'

'I don't know,' and then, 'I'm seeing Matron

about it at nine-thirty tomorrow morning.'

'Are you now! She'll want you to stay on. She hates letting go of good nurses, and I suppose you can't blame her for that. At the same time it might be an idea to go to pastures new for a bit.'

'Only I haven't any pastures new in my world. I have been so occupied with the hospital and getting through the exams, and all the rest of it, that I have had no time to get an eye on a pasture new. Tomorrow I shall book in for the next two years, I bet.'

Frank Dene looked at her with calm, grey eyes. He was one of those men who instinctively *know* things. An understanding man, who had had but one affair with a girl in all his life (so the others told her). He said, 'Has Master Edgar been playing you up?'

'Oh no! We have been good friends, no more,' and then, in a burst of foolish confession, 'I thought ... perhaps tonight. ... We waited till I got through the exams, there comes a time in your life when nothing but those beastly exams matter, for everything depends on them. ...' She hesitated.

'Yes, of course. I do understand. Take a bit of advice from someone much older than yourself. Age looks pretty silly when you are twenty, I know, but sometimes age has been kicked hard enough to beware of further kickings. If I were you I should get away for a bit. Right away. Why not take a private job for three months? It would give you time to think, and that is what you want most. Time to find your feet.'

'Would it be fair to Matron?'

'I should not bother myself too much about Matron. The mother hospital will always get you back into the fold later on if you want to come back, so that need not bother you. But I *should* get away for a few weeks. Truly you *should* get away.'

'And lose him for ever,' she half-whispered, as Edgar whirled past them, with Nelly's cheek against his own; both of them were plainly enjoying every single moment of it.

When she could speak again, Bridget said, 'I can't go anywhere else, for the ordinary reason that I have nowhere to go!'

'I see.'

'It *is* a complication, you know.'

'Of course, but not a very lasting one. I wonder if I could tempt you with an idea? I happen to have a friend who lives in Cornwall. It's a fine county.'

He paused, and in that moment she recalled pictures she had once seen of Land's End, of the Cornish coast, of the gaunt stern hills and the harsh rocks, of the crystal clear sea at Falmouth, and the sands of Sennen Cove.

'Cornwall is heaven,' she whispered.

'It is the most amazing county in England. Things still happen there.' He warmed to his subject, and suddenly he became one of the most interesting men she had ever met. 'They say the "little people" were kicked out of England, and retreated nearer and nearer to the sea, and some of them were left there in Cornwall and still live there. They grant wishes. I can speak because they granted mine once. It is a county of adventure, everything happens there; it is a wonderful county.'

'It—it sounds like it,' she said, and knew that somehow he had pulled her out of herself. A picture had come into her heart; of Land's End with a high sea beating round it, and the rock known as the Silent Knight sprawling out into the angry sea.

He said, 'You must know my friend's name, she writes books. Damned good ones, and is a best-seller of the highest degree! She is Gay Sutcliffe.'

'Not *the* Gay Sutcliffe?'

'Indeed, yes. She has never married, poor lamb. I know that somewhere in her history a dream lingers. There was a lover who died. But she adores Cornwall, and she lives there to write her books. She has an amazing house almost in the sea. Once it belonged to the wreckers.'

'The wreckers?'

'Memories of a hundred years back, or more. They lay in wait to raid ships approaching the shore with precious cargo, cargo that was worth money. Then they changed the lights and did other misleading things, and so caused the ships

24

to founder and yield up their booty.'

'What happened to the crews?'

'I'm afraid a lot of them went west! The wreckers were dreaded more than anything else along that coast, that is a cert!'

'Are they still going?'

'Good God, no! What do you suppose our coastguards are for? But let's get back to my friend. Poor old thing! For years she has been badly crippled by rheumatoid arthritis. At times she is just hunched up with it, then it gets better for a bit, and she starts a new book. She always has to have a nurse with her.'

The first light dawned on Bridget, and she could hardly believe that it was true. 'You don't mean. . . ?'

He went on talking. One thing about Frank Dene was that usually he was a quiet man, but when he began to chat he never left off. He spoke of Gay Sutcliffe. 'For years she has been stuck this way, always with a nurse with her. The one she has now has had a bit of a breakdown and needs a month's holiday right away. I am trying to find the right girl to take her place, and you would be right for it, Bridget. She is a pet; the pay is good, and I should have said that it is the most divine countryside in England.'

'But could I do it?'

'Of *course* you could! The local doctor is something of a drip, ex-R.N., but there is really little one can do for the patient, and she is so nice.'

Bridget thought it over for a few moments. She thought again of the vivid pictures she had seen of Cornwall, St. Michael's Mount, St. Ives, Land's End, and the derelict tin mines whose closure had brought disaster to the county. She said, 'I must say Cornwall has always fascinated me.'

He spoke quietly, 'Look here. It is not often that life holds out a helpful hand, but this is exactly what it is doing to you now. At this identical moment. Here and now. She lives in a strange old house, which is almost in the sea, and keeps a lavish board. You must be sick to death of hospital food, and you'd love each other.'

'I'd never get the job.'

He laughed at that, then he said, 'She'd take anyone I recommended, I can promise you that. I do think you are the right girl for this, and I want you to go down there. Cornwall is a wonderful county.'

'I . . . I have always wanted to go there. The moor is a bit spooky, so I'm told.'

'A bit, but the house where Gay lives is a dream.'

'Wreckers and all?'

'Oh, she got rid of practically all the traces of them. Think about it, Bridget. I believe that this chance has come into your life at this very moment because Fate wants you to go there.'

'You believe in Fate?'

'What Cornishman does not? Now, come on, and get some supper before it is all eaten up.'

She was in a daze now. It was as though some absurd fairy had waved a wand and her whole world had changed. One of those things which one cannot believe is true, because it is too amazing.

The supper room was clearing off a little, and there was no difficulty in finding a corner table. The room resounded with the pop of champagne corks, and with laughter. It was one of those dances! Bridget might be sentimental about the hospital where she had trained, but she kept telling herself that this was not the time to think of Matron's feelings, but of her own. Most girls would grab at this lovely idea.

He made her drink champagne to cheer her up, though she did not drink normally. He recommended the little cold partridges and the pheasant pie. He had discernment for the good things of this life.

'It must all of it be tinned,' she said.

'Does that matter, if it tastes good?' He had something there. They talked of hospital, of its scandals, its chatter, and about a new treatment being tried out here about which there were qualms, but great hope also. Here was Edgar Thorn as large as life, sitting on a sofa seat with his pretty little partner beside him.

'That young fellow makes the most of his time,' said Frank, 'and he gets a lot of fun, but this never deters him. He is not the sort prepared to give everything up for a patient; he likes fun, and he is getting it now. He ought to outgrow it.'

'He enjoys it,' she said.

'Yes,' and he laughed. 'Maybe he is one of those chaps who later look back on ravishing salad days, and wonder what on earth happened to stop the fun lasting. Nobody can make the fun last, alas, however much they want to put a brake on time.'

'I know.'

'He isn't the kind that grow up well.'

'I wonder.' She could not imagine Edgar growing up in the full sense of the words. Maybe she had gone a trifle quiet; this was a sore subject. It was quite plain to anyone who had the eyes to see, that Edgar Thorn would never outgrow the flirtatious take-your-fun-whilst-you-can-get-it stage, and he pursued this in complete disregard of whatever others thought of him. She wished she could now concentrate on Frank and the wonderful job that he had suggested for her, but she kept glancing across to where Edgar sat with Nelly, just to see how things were going. And they *were* going, for he was that sort of man.

Just before she finally parted from Frank Dene, who had been kindness itself, he made her promise to give him an answer tomorrow, after she had seen Matron.

'And don't go committing yourself to her silly suggestions,' he said. 'Of course she wants to keep a good nurse at home with her, in her own hospital. She'll play her cards good and hearty, but don't you be taken in for a single moment. Just stand firm. A few weeks away from hospital would do you all the good in the world, and this is a super job.'

She looked up with a smile. Perhaps the first time she had thought of smiling since she had come to the dance. 'I think I shall take the job,' she said. 'I just think. . . .'

'That's the girl!' he said.

Edgar came for her, four dances later.

'I've been a bit caught up, my darling,' said he, with something of a forced brightness.

'I'll say you have!'

'Don't be angry with me. Nelly is a sweet piece, but what her dad can do for me would be far sweeter. Now I am here, and dancing with my own girl.'

'I'm not so sure that I am going to be your own girl any more,' she said, surprised at the defiance in her tone.

'Good Lord! Who would have thought that you would be so misunderstanding?'

'Misunderstanding my foot!' She had got the bit between her teeth by now.

'What's changed you?'

29

'I'm seeing Matron in the morning.'

'Yes, of course, all you girls do. And she will offer you a belt and an appointment for two years, and you'll take it. Then we shall see a lot of each other, and have the loveliest times.' He pressed her hand closer, and laid his cheek against her own.

You would have thought that this would have enchanted her, it always had until now, but now she had changed. She was furious with him. He was the man who licked all the icing off the cake of life, and then very quietly went off to pastures new, when there was only the stale old cake itself left to him.

She said, 'I'm taking a job in Cornwall.'

That shook him. She felt the whole of his body quiver, and he nearly tripped up, unusual for him, for he was a very good dancer. 'What the devil do you mean?'

'I've been offered the pearl of jobs. Someone ill in Cornwall, a very famous woman, and you know her name well. Her own nurse has to go away on holiday and she wants a temporary.' She gave a little laugh, it was a moment of exultation to see how dismayed he was. He was a man who gloried in doing exactly this to other people, and now it was coming his way. His face dropped. 'I shall get four times the money I have ever had before, and four times the fun, and I'm taking it. Grabbing it, with both hands.'

30

He stared at her as though he had suddenly had his pocket picked and every penny he possessed had gone with it. Then he said, 'It can't be true! You wouldn't be such a fool. Every girl serves her two years here after qualifying.'

'I shall come back to serve mine, but for now I am having something of a holiday, and a very paying one, in the loveliest part of England.'

'It shows you don't know! All those withered tin mines, all that rocky coast, the lifeboat goes out every night. You're going to regret this. You stand on the edge of making the biggest fool of yourself that could be.'

She said the one thing that she had never supposed she would dare to say to him, but it came. 'Not half as much of a fool as I should have been if I had stayed on here hoping you would suggest marriage, when all the time you never meant anything of the kind,' said she, and calmly walked away.

He had never had this happen to him before. She knew it instantly by the way he looked, by the horror in his eyes, by the sheer end-of-the-world appearance of everything about him.

But he did not follow her.

She had a last dance with the gynaecologist, who was a lively fellow off duty, but sour as they come when on. She stood for the National Anthem, and went up to her little dog-hole of a room with the feeling that she walked on air!

The whole world had changed, and she would have been a fool not to grab at the answer.

'This has been the greatest night of all my life,' she told herself, and she slept like a top.

CHAPTER TWO

Bridget slept late. She had just crawled into bed, unable to keep her eyes open, and now she woke after the bell had gone. At one time she had told herself that nobody in the world could go on sleeping when that noisy croaky bell went, but one gets used to anything.

Nowadays she never even heard it, and often had to be rapped up by one of the Sisters who had not seen her go down, and suspected the worst. She woke with that sick uncertain feeling of being a girl who just could not go through with the coming day. Living would ask too much of her.

She went to the dining-room, and the rest of them were halfway through, which always gave the place a far more depressing look than usual. It was fish morning; one knew it before one ever approached the dining-room, and one squirmed from it. She felt a little sick. There was no doubt about it, festivities of the kind she had had last night were not the best possible things for nurses who had a hard day's work to do. She had toast and marmalade. The toast was leathery; here it really was the case of 'first come first served', and it was her own fault for oversleeping. She drank down tepid coffee, and remembered that she would have to go back for a cleaner apron in which to interview Matron. Such a visit asked everything to be spruce, and there was no hope of Matron not noticing anything the slightest bit wrong.

She bolted back to her room.

Then she came downstairs, with time to spare. She went down the quiet corridor which led to Matron's office. Two young nurses were sitting on the small bench put outside for this purpose. Both were spruced-up with never a hair awry, and that sort of look about them which disclosed that they were scared stiff, but not for the world they show it. They glanced apprehensively at Bridget. Then a voice from within called, and one of them went inside.

'Now she's for it,' said the other.

'What has she been doing?'

'Oh, the good old usual. She got locked out. There is a most convenient lamp-post which leads up to her first floor dorm. Something went wrong. A lot of bricks had been delivered the day before, she never knew that they were there and in the end had to wake up the porter.'

'Hard luck!'

'Yes,' sighed the other.

But apparently Matron was in a good mood,

for the girl shot through and came out again not looking too worried. Her friend went next; after all, they had been here first. She also was as quick; then Bridget went in. Matron was far younger than most of them, a woman with a clear pink skin, and a pile of rich, brown hair, almost chestnut. She smiled encouragingly.

'Nice to see you, Nurse; so you came through the examinations, and now has come the moment when we consider your future career.'

'Yes, Matron.'

'We like to keep our girls here. Some of our older Sisters were trained here and that is the way that we prefer it.'

'Yes, Matron.'

'We would be very happy now, for you to go into the wards in the usual manner.' She glanced down at the papers at her side. 'I have very agreeable reports of your work here, and your behaviour when on duty.'

'Thank you, Matron.'

There came a moment's pause, then Matron, possibly realizing the fact that there was something doubtful in the tone of voice, looked across at her. 'You—you have something else you wished to say to me, Nurse?'

'If you please, Matron.'

'What is it?'

'Before I finally settle down here, I should have liked to have a change. Perhaps three months away in private nursing, or something like that. A chance to see the world I—I have lived a very sheltered life, and have seen very little of anything outside my job. I feel this could be the only opportunity I might get, and I, well, I have been offered a job.'

'A job?' Matron's eyebrows went up a quarter of an inch; everyone here knew that she liked the girls to get straight on with the work, not go elsewhere. She did not want them to see the world (and in the doing of this, perhaps earn themselves quite a lot of experience which might be disconcerting). She said, 'And what sort of a job is it?'

'She is an authoress living in Cornwall, and her own nurse is going on holiday; she needs someone *pro tem*. It is an arthritis case.'

'You mean Miss Gay Sutcliffe?'

She did, of course. Perhaps she had forgotten the friendship between Frank and Matron, and it was likely that they had discussed this case between them.

'Yes, Matron.'

'It's a long way off.'

'Yes, Matron, but I have always longed to see Cornwall.'

'I have always longed to see India, but I doubt if I would allow that longing to come between me and my career,' and Matron said it in that icy voice of hers, at which she was so proficient.

'No, Matron.'

'You are quite sure this is what you wish?'

She was *quite* sure, and she said so. There was another of those rather painful lulls which were so terrifying. Matron had the high art of scaring people stiff, and did it without a doubt most effectively.

'I would not wish to stand in your way, but it is unusual for a girl to leave us after she has availed herself of everything that the hospital offers to her to get through her exams and qualify. Apparently you do not wish to do this. But you have overworked, according to your reports, and a change might help you. At the end of that time. . . ?' She glanced at Bridget.

'I would be grateful to return, if the hospital wanted me, Matron,' she said, but quietly.

'I will remember that.' Matron had a tremendous genius for appearing to be quite unmoved. She held out her hand, 'Good morning, Nurse.'

'Good morning, Matron.'

Somehow she had not thought that it would be quite as bad as this. She had never supposed that Matron could for a moment object, for a third of the girls who qualified here had by the moment they were through had so much of the hospital that their one idea had been to get right away. She went out of the room into the outer room, then into the corridor. Two other girls were sitting there, and the one nearer the door rose with alacrity.

'Oh, God, now it's me!' she said.

Walking along the corridor, and turning at the far end into the main part of the great hospital, Bridget was thinking that whatever happened she had got the thought of Cornwall ahead. Thousands of girls would have given their all to escape to a lovely county like Cornwall, and to a job with a novelist as famous as Gay Sutcliffe. It opened the door on to tremendous possibilities. Now she would get all the arrangements made.

They took precious little time, really.

She spoke on the 'phone to the house down in Cornwall, and she found Miss Sutcliffe's secretary a most charming person. They hoped she could come down this week, Thursday would be an excellent day, and she promised this. Miss Sutcliffe had already posted a cheque to her in advance. She felt sure that there were small purchases that she would want to make. In the main Miss Sutcliffe was not too keen on her wearing uniform all the time, she felt it looked wrong in a private house, and therefore she hoped that Bridget would find time suitably to equip her wardrobe. Could anything be more charming?

The secretary was most helpful. She assured Bridget that she would be one of the luckiest girls, for there was little real work attached to the job; the patient had her bad days of course, but she had good ones as well. It was a glorious part of the world, not far from Land's End and

37

with all manner of exciting spots to visit. When she rang off, Bridget was enchanted.

The cheque came, and she went out and began to spend it.

Never in the whole of her life had she ever been able to buy so freely. A couple of cottons, each with a tiny coatee, and a sort of party dress for dinner at home.

She saw Edgar Thorn as she returned from shopping. He had come into the courtyard where all the doctors kept their cars; he went to his own (an extravagant model, but then he came from an extravagant family). Purposely she pretended not to see him, for she had felt badly about the dance, and the way he had behaved. She had been so confident that he really had something to say to her, the very words which she most wanted to hear, then little Nelly Stein had come along and had ended the affair.

But if she hoped to avoid him now, she was wrong. He saw her, turned instantly and called to her.

'Bridget?'

This time she pretended not to hear. There was no point in hearing what he had to say, and she hastened slightly. He must have come after her, for the next thing she knew was that he was alongside her and that his hand gripped her wrist.

'What's the matter with you, and where are

you off to, I'd like to know? Darling, what's the worry? I hardly saw you at the dance.'

'And you know why, don't you?'

'I liked her, and her father could do a lot for me.'

'And you *did* help *her!*'

He still held on to her wrist, and she wished to goodness that the fingers did not close so firmly, and also that they could not madden her.

He said, 'Don't be a silly little idiot! That sort of dance means that you have to look after all the strange girls, and lose touch with your own true love.'

'You said you had something to say to me.'

'I'll say it now. Come into the car, and we'll go somewhere into the country to sup. It's a glorious night, one of the sweetest that summer can give us; it would be an awful pity to miss it.'

She did not budge an inch.

'I have qualified, as you know.'

'I was sure you would.'

'I'm not settling in here for months waiting until I can go higher in the world. I need a change, and I have taken the job in Cornwall. You won't be seeing me again for a long time.'

'But what on earth will you do in Cornwall? A hospital in Truro probably, or one of those very slick nursing homes they have in Penzance where all the old dowagers go to die, and then get themselves buried in their pearl necklaces!'

'Most certainly *not!*' she answered.

'Then what are you going to do?'

'Frank Dene was something of a help.'

'He's never been that to me!' and he laughed. 'I always felt that he had a weakness for women.'

'It was nothing of that sort.' She felt herself growing angry, and only hoped that she did not show it.

The truth of the matter was that she should have realized a very long time ago that Edgar Thorn might be wildly attractive, and a hero as a lover, but he was *not* reliable. Sister Tutor had said rather sadly, 'Girls who marry men like that young man, suffer for it severely. I can tell you that, so don't be misled by a load of good looks, a ravishing manner, a father with money, and a lot of pretty compliments.'

But the main bother in life is that one *is* led astray this way. Now Edgar stood before her, tall, elegant, not a single extra ounce on him, with the sort of figure grand young gentlemen have, thick hair on the brow, and dancing, laughing eyes.

'What's come over you, my sweet? The dance was a party, and everyone has fun at a party.'

'I didn't,' she said, and maybe that was the bitter truth. She had *not* enjoyed it. She had expected to go to bed that night engaged to this very young man. The absurd part was that she loved him. It was ridiculous, but she had been so sure of him. Others had warned her, but is

40

there ever a handsome young man in the world whom people do not warn a girl against?

'Let's make it tonight,' he said, 'and I won't take no for an answer.'

'I'm not coming with you, Edgar, I've had enough.'

'All because of a little piece like Nelly, whose dad could do a lot for me; and because you are furious with me.'

If it hadn't been for that 'little piece like Nelly', there would never have been this scene this morning. Everything the hospital had ever said about Edgar Thorn was true. He *was* vivacious, flirtatious and a man you could not trust. She said, 'Other people warned me about you.'

'I bet they did! Has there ever been a man you have not been warned against? and more especially in hospitals. All those catty old Sisters who only came into the service with the idea of marrying into Harley Street and living like fighting cocks, or hens!'

'That isn't true.'

He said, 'I know I let you down. I know the whole evening slipped the wrong way, but I got caught up in a net from which I could not disentangle myself. That was that, but it is all behind us now. Come and sup with me tonight at the Blue Peacock at eight sharp?'

The Blue Peacock was one of the better restaurants, where at times one saw the specialists, where Matron had been seen, in a dazzling evening dress, and looking quite unlike herself. 'No, thank you,' she said and turned away.

It was a dismal night. The other girls were still talking hard about the wonderful times they had had, the dance of a lifetime, and their wild successes with different young gentlemen, and this and that, whilst she went stoically about her work. When tackled, she said she had a bad headache. Anything not to discuss it, for surely some of them must have noticed Edgar's behaviour? and like a fool she had murmured something about tonight being *the* night, which had given quite different ideas.

She was at lunch next day when she was called to the telephone in the great hall. Mercifully, at this time of day there was not that continuous tide of comings and goings, which could be confusing. During this one hour it could be entirely empty. She shut herself in the box, half afraid that Edgar Thorn had had the cheek to ring her up here. But it was a woman at the far end, a voice coming through clearly, though on a long-distance call.

'I am Hilda Grey, secretary to Miss Gay Sutcliffe, I am speaking from Cornwall. Miss Sutcliffe wants a word with you.'

'Oh yes, of course.'

She waited a moment, half afraid that if she was not careful the dream would fall through.

Horror gripped hold of her. Perhaps after all it had been too good to be true, and she gasped to herself.

Then from the other end there came the pretty, very gentle voice of the woman who wrote books. 'This is Gay Sutcliffe speaking. I thought maybe you would like to hear my voice, and I wanted to hear your yours. I hope you will be very happy here.'

'I'm sure I shall be, Miss Sutcliffe.'

'I understand you have never been to Cornwall before. It is a curious county, quite unlike any other in England, and most exciting. I hope you will enjoy being here.'

'I'm sure I shall. And I very much hope that I can be of real help to you.'

'I know you will be. I get hunches, and I have a hunch about you.'

'I'm so glad.'

She spoke then of the house which she had restored and made livable after it had almost collapsed. It was a comfortable house to work in, with all the modern amenities, something of everything. There were lovely drives around, pleasant bathing and nice neighbours. She would now hand her back to her secretary who had a list of suitable trains and could guide her as to the best way to come.

'Thank you so much.'

The secretary seemed to be completely able to carry things through and to fix everything up.

She suggested the train leaving Paddington at eleven in the morning; it was a fast train, and one could get a good lunch on board.

She casually mentioned again the fact that Miss Sutcliffe was not too keen on her nurse wearing uniform. 'She hates being reminded of the fact that she is ill, and unless she is really bad she would prefer you to wear plain clothes. This is what the cheque was for, and your ticket down here.'

Three pips started to make themselves heard. A second later there was Bridget standing staring at the rather musty little wall of the telephone booth and knowing that her immediate future was decided and finally settled.

There was no going back now even with the wild hope of making Edgar Thorn change his bad ways, and actually flirt with her. It was silly to have been in love with him, and Sister Tutor had kept telling her so, but when you are deeply in love with the most handsome man in the building, how can you listen to reason?

It was Frank Dene who put her mind finally at rest. He had known Gay Sutcliffe well since he was about twelve years old, and she had always given him the best tip of the lot with which to return to school. 'Don't worry about cheques from her, for she has the biggest and most generous heart in all the world. A proper spoiler,' was the way he put it. 'What's more, she loves seeing people pleasantly dressed about her. She likes gay frocks.'

She went out again and did some more shopping. It was almost as if a fairy godmother had waved a wand and the world had turned to magic. It was all the more magic because never before had she been able to buy the things that she really wanted. Now she was enjoying herself so much.

Tonight she put on one of the new dresses to go out to eat with Frank Dene, again at the Blue Peacock. She knew that it was expensive, but she appreciated that it offered a lot more for the money than the usual rather seedy little café. It would ask a better dress, and the extraordinary thing was that for the first time in her life she had several dresses from which she could choose. The choice fell on the little party dress she had bought, a soft blue, with a deep sash, and she knew that somehow the dress did something to her.

She got to the restaurant a trifle late, for there had been taxi trouble. As she had a purse full of money, she did not bother, and that was a delightful situation, and she had taken a taxi.

The outside of the restaurant warned her that it was slick. The windows were delicately draped with cream curtains, and one stepped inside into an elegant little entrance hall, with a green carpet and comfortable chairs. There were few people sitting about because as yet it was early. She would have slid into a corner seat out of the way as she had no wish to be obvious, when a head waiter appeared.

'Madam is waiting for someone?'

'Yes, I am the guest of Mr. Frank Dene.'

'Yes, Madam, this way please.'

He led her into an inner room, with a different atmosphere. There were yellow roses on the tables; she did not know why this struck her quite so forcefully, but it did. She had always loved yellow roses ever since as a child she had watched a *gloire de Dijon* pressing its lovely blooms against her nursery windows. Somehow it seemed that her early life had been influenced by those soft yellow flowers.

'You're delightfully punctual,' Frank said, 'and what a pretty dress!'

'My new employer sent me the money for it.'

'Gay is like that; she adores buying things for other people. You two are going to like each other quite enormously, let me tell you. Have a drink?'

'I don't drink, thank you.'

'A T.T. one then? Bitter lemon, tonic water, something like that?'

She chose a bitter lemon.

He talked of a house offered to him in Harley Street only yesterday, but for the moment he was not sure that he had sufficient influence to dare to start in Harley Street. He also had his own worries, but, as he admitted, if one wished to get along in the medical world, then one had to have a consulting-room in that holy of holies.

She nodded.

'And when do you go down to Cornwall?'

'On Thursday.'

'How like Gay! She loves doing things at speed; at first it may worry you, but you will soon get used to it. She is a charming, spontaneous person, and does things on the spur of the moment. I doubt if anyone could suffer as much as she has suffered, poor lamb.'

'I hope to be of some use to her.'

'I hope you will. She is at times very lonely.'

'She should have married.'

'If I were you, I should be careful what you say about that sort of thing, for she is a curious woman, and of course she should have married. She was a very beautiful woman once; even now in the fifties she is still beautiful, I always think, but she works herself to death at her job. You may be able to get her interested in outside things, for that is what ought to happen. She gets too concerned about the things which are immediately around her.'

'Yes, I can see that.'

'She should go out and about more, but gets worried that she will get a bad attack, and this complaint of hers hurts like mad, as you can imagine.'

'Yes, I know.'

'I am sure you will be able to do something for

her which others have failed to do, and you are just the kind she likes most. She—she has a boyfriend there for the moment. . . .' His voice trailed off.

'A *boyfriend*, did you say?'

'Yes, and I feel his interest is very alien to her. He is a very good-looking sort of chap, dark (she likes them dark), with highly intelligent eyes. Do what you can for her, and make her as comfortable as possible. We all know that this wretched arthritis is damned painful, and therefore it can and does scare her. But at any hour a cure could be found, for they are getting near to it in the labs, but half of her despairs. Try to convince her that it will work out one of these days.'

'I will try,' she said.

'She is the kindest person in all the world. Takes up protégés. It's Julian Clare for the moment; she calls him her adopted nephew. You ought to get rid of him, for I am not too keen on the fellow. He's nice enough, and gay enough, but I always feel there is something about him which is unpleasant.'

'And acts as bodyguard?'

'He does indeed. You must say you like him, for half the time Gay adores him; she is very lonely, poor thing, and badly needs a happier form of existence; this business would wear anyone down. Be good to her, and she will do anything for you, I promise you that.'

He changed the subject then, and talked instead of the Cornish countryside, which in Gay's neighbourhood was at its most beautiful. It was an attractive world of amazing wild flowers which grew everywhere, of piskies and fairies, so he said. At Zennor there was a mermaid who came to church on one Sunday in the year, flapping her tail across the meadows to her seat in the church; she had a special seat kept for her. It was also rumoured by gossips that when she went back to sea she always took some boy with her. She was the mermaid who loved boyfriends, and came to Zennor church to sneak one out of the choir! You would have thought that the parents and the parson would together attack her, for she had these funny habits, but nobody accomplished anything. For years she never appeared, so the old verger said, even though they had a special chair put into the church to receive her, known as 'The Mermaid's Chair'. He fondly believed in her. No, he agreed, he hadn't never seen her really, but only her shadow in the porch, and had heard the thud of her tail as she went off later on.

'But it's true!' he said. 'Oh yes, there's no doubt about it, it's true.'

Frank laughed and said he had always been delighted by the story, and the fact that nobody had ever actually seen her, but every choirboy lived in sheer dread of her.

'I shall come down to see you,' Frank told

her, 'for I love that part of the world, with the spooks and the fairies and the ghosties. I go there every year several times, and enjoy it. I hate that awful journey over Salisbury Plain; why doesn't someone buy it and turn it into a garden city? But I promise you I *shall* come down to see you.'

Somehow she knew that this would come true.

He *would* come and see her, and she would be enchanted to have him with her. It was on his advice that she bought one or two small things to take with her. One was a good leather case, for she had a lot to pack for this journey, with her initials on it, and a good overcoat which one always wanted in the country. It was a cream, woollen French coat, with just that wee bit of difference which showed a purchaser whence it came. She had decided to travel light. It was going to be a very long trip, and she was told that the first part of it was incredibly dull; it was only when you first saw the deep red soil of Devonshire that you appreciated that the best part of the journey lay before you.

Frank said, 'You're a wise girl to go. You are only young once; make the most of the happy days when legs don't get tired, and heads don't start to ache, because they never come back in quite the same way. You'll adore Devon when the train gets you there; you'll find Cornwall more gaunt, more rugged, but a place of even greater character.'

'It's going to be a dream come true.'

'That's the idea!' he told her.

The waiter brought the coffee meringues. Surely one of the loveliest sweets in all the world, so she told herself. That was the way she felt tonight, out with one of the most understanding men she knew, and such a help.

At the end of the evening she knew that she had never enjoyed a dinner more, and she stood on the threshold of tomorrow. When they said good night, she felt entirely at ease against this setting. He repeated that he would come down to visit her. 'I shall look forward to it,' she said.

★   ★   ★

She would never forget leaving the hospital, and she had the impression that she was leaving it for ever. It was the same old dreary breakfast, the same old good-byes to girls on duty, and they had to hurry. In a way Bridget was glad, because she hated good-byes, somehow they seemed to be all wrong.

The dining-room emptied, and she went out of it herself, perhaps for the last time. 'I'm getting doleful,' she told herself, 'and this is all wrong when I stand on the very edge of a great adventure, maybe the first really exciting one of all my life.' She would miss all this, for somehow now she was part of the pattern of the

51

place, and it would not be easy to cut herself adrift. But she had wanted to break free.

She looked at the pretty new dress, and the clean white lace collar. She was a new person.

A probationer spoke to her in the passage. 'So you're off on the great adventure? I do wish you luck, and all the best.'

'I'll be back later on.'

'Unless you lose your heart to Cornwall. Some people do.'

'I know. But perhaps I—I don't lose my heart very easily,' and she laughed.

A bell rang and sent the probationer off on her duty.

Bridget took her luggage to the door. She got there at the same moment as a taxi deposited a doctor there, and she got in and went to Paddington. The journey had started, the big journey, and she knew that she was thrilled. There was the whirl of Paddington station, getting her seat in the train, and curling up in a corner. She had bought two morning papers and they held her attention as far as Reading. Then it was lunch time and she went to the dining-car. She did not hurry, for she wanted to kill time, and the train was now racing over Salisbury Plain; they made good time, for it was one of the crack trains of the day. She went back to her seat.

They were at Exeter when she came to. She had slept a little, for excitement can make a girl sleepy. Now Devonshire was round her, not as thrilling as she had expected, and they entered Cornwall. Three people left the carriage, and she dozed off. It was late when she awoke to a country of slate roofs, of blue seas, and scattered rocks. The man opposite looked at her. He laid down his copy of *The Farmer's Weekly*, and she got the idea that he looked like a farmer.

He said, 'Your first visit here?'

'Yes, it is. I'm going to the Wreckers' House.'

'I live near there. You're the nurse going to be with Miss Sutcliffe, aren't you?'

'Yes, I am. How did you know?'

'My farm is very close to her house, and news travels fast in this part of the world.' The blue eyes smiled. He was a sturdy type of man with light hair and very bright eyes.

'Is it very far?' she asked.

'Very little way now. My farm comes first.'

She would have thought that he was of Cornish stock, and somehow she felt instinctively that they liked each other. He glanced over to where she was sitting.

'What do you think of Cornwall so far?'

'Already I love it.'

She saw that his eyes brightened, and there came something of a blue flame in them. He was a man who obviously loved the rugged countryside, and the cliffs so assailed by the battering seas, so exposed, yet with deliciously sunny beaches. There were woods where the

53

rhododendrons turned them so rosy that you could not see the green. That was when the first migrating birds returned home.

They talked as if they had known each other for years. She thought that he would be ten years older than she, and a farmer. In fact, he had said that he lived next to the house where Gay Sutcliffe lived.

'You'll love it, I'll guarantee that. My farm is only a quarter of a mile from her house, and we meet most days. She is a great reader, and I lend her books.'

She remembered what Frank Dene had said, about the man who lived in the farm that his family had inherited for generations and who had one of the finest libraries in the county. 'Your name is Alan Thane?' she said. 'Mine is Bridget Smythe, and I am coming down here to help her, or so I hope.'

'She is a darling.'

'I'm sure she is.'

'Her adopted nephew, Julian Clare, is with her at the moment, and he will show you the routine.'

'Is he charming, too?'

It seemed for a single second that a look passed over her companion's face, a look which betrayed nothing, yet everything, something that she did not understand. Then he said, 'Yes, of course. He is not a relative really. Poor Gay, she is singularly alone in the world, one of those people who have fought their own fight, and at times must have been very lonely. I go to see her most days, so we shall meet often. I know it will make me very happy. Cornwall during the winter months is a deserted county, only those who have been born there seem to live there right through. But when spring comes again, then the crowds return. There will be a lot of them soon. Already they are beginning. Weekends, and there are visitors. By midsummer they are here all the time.'

'I am sure I shall love it.'

As they neared the small station (for since she had got into a smaller train, most of them had been mere wayside halts), he said, 'I expect you are being met. Julian Clare will have brought the car for you. I'll hang around just for a moment in case he is late or anything, but I don't imagine there will be any trouble.'

She collected her small dressing-case. She was glad that she had bought that one smart piece of luggage, for she knew that the trunk in the guard's van was anything but smart. Today people had such lovely modern cases, she would have liked one, but somehow she knew that for now she must go slowly.

The train drew to a standstill at a small countrified station. There were dying lupins and budding delphiniums in the border, a tree of fat, red roses, with the most amazing blooms in the world, she thought. 'I am going to like this,' she told herself impulsively, and as the train drew to a rather chattering standstill, 'I am going to love it.'

CHAPTER THREE

Alan Thane helped her out of the carriage, it was quite a long drop down on to the platform, with light dust under feet. At that very moment she saw another man approaching her; he had come out of the waiting-room where the guard was standing (or a man who she imagined was the guard) with a country flower saucily stuck into his cap.

The new young man was, if anything, a trifle over-dressed. He wore fawn-coloured trousers so well pressed that as far as she could see he had only just bought them. The shirt was the same colour, and the cravat an exquisite piece of silk, pale blue and brown, a glorious mixture of colours. He came towards them.

'Hello, Thane! So you got there first!' and he laughed. 'This must be Nurse?'

'I've arrived safely,' she said with a smile.

Julian Clare was a shade too polished, she told herself; he had dark eyes, and she had always felt that with most men dark eyes hid their secrets. It is far more difficult to read the truth behind dark eyes than behind light ones.

The men spoke for a moment, then Julian Clare took over her case and they went outside into the very countrified little yard in front of the station. Now she saw standing there, an immaculate car. It was the sort that only very rich and very young men drive. A radiant car, in light tan with darker tan leather fittings, and luxury in every line of it. 'What a miracle of a car!' she said.

'Gay gave it to me. She spoils me. She is really the most magnificent person, and I adore her. So will you when you meet her.'

'Is the house far away?'

'Three miles, and through good old Cornish country. You can smell the sea from here.' She took in a deep breath and she did smell it. It was the salty scent which she had loved as a child on those occasions when her people took her to the shore. She saw the countryside, a farm here and there, sheep, a light mist, and in the distance the outline of a hill.

'It's heaven here,' she said.

'Heaven, and a bit more for luck.'

Now she saw the sea ahead, greenish blue, almost as if one could see through it and pierce down into it, a new sea, a sea that might be aquamarine, not turquoise, for this had a quality of crystal in it. One could see through it.

He said, 'That farm over there is where Alan Thane lives, I'd say the most prosperous farm in the neighbourhood; he must make a fortune, as his people did before him, dozens of them, and they all did well. I'd swop with him even if I have a fairy godmother in the shape of Gay, and she is a pet.'

Now she saw the house, in the dip close to the water's edge. A big, rambling, old house, with outhouses beyond it, giving the appearance of storehouses, some blackened by time. There were tubs of flowers standing before it, giving the gay impression of beauty and of happiness. She could not associate the word 'wreckers' with it, it was so pretty, nestling close to the water, and with that crystal clear sea in palest blue lying beyond it. Bridget felt elated that she had come here, for it was quite one of the most lovely places she had ever seen. How fortunate she was! Here she could forget.

'I never thought it could be so lovely,' she told Julian Clare as they drew up alongside the heavy front door.

'I said it was heaven.'

'I know you did, but forgive me if I took this with a grain of salt.'

They went up the three shallow steps, and he brought out a key to open the door, but before he had managed to get it in the lock, Janet the housekeeper (she must have been waiting for them) had done it herself. She was a compact little woman in the fifties, her grey hair snugly drawn back from a rosy apple of a face, with bright eyes.

'Welcome to you both,' she said, and smiled.

Behind her lay a great hall, with polished floor, crimson rugs, and wide stairs slowly mounting upwards at the far end. It was a much larger house than she had anticipated, beautifully kept, the sort of house in which it would be a sheer joy to live. Tea was on the table in the corner.

'Some tea first?' Janet suggested.

Possibly it was the magnificent iced cake which caught at her heart! She went over to the tea table and sat down. She knew that the luggage was being brought in and taken upstairs, and that this was all far more impressive than she had ever thought possible. The great hall could once have been a wreckers' barn, but it had outlived that wild time and was now surprisingly serene and lovely. In the end Julian Clare joined her.

'This happens to be one of poor Gay's bad days. They come just when you don't want them, of course, and this is one of them. We'll have tea, and then you have a rest and get changed, and after dinner perhaps she will be better. It is a strange thing, but it always seems to get better towards the end of the day.'

'Yes, of course.'

Perhaps he suspected her thoughts, for he enquired, 'This is not quite the sort of house that you expected?'

'I did not think it would be so big, so

remarkable, or so interesting.'

He patted her arm. 'Now the thing to do is to forget all that. Have a good tea, nip upstairs, unpack, have a sleep if you can. These tiresomely long journeys are always far *too* long. But the tea should refresh you, and I must say I have never tasted cakes like them. They are perfect.' Julian was a nice man, most anxious to help her, and then when she had done he took her up the ancestral staircase, along the corridor to her room. It was the most beautiful room that she was ever likely to have.

'But it's tremendous,' she said.

'Don't worry. The bell is connected with Gay's room. You can ring each other at any time. That's just in case something goes wrong.'

When he had gone, she examined everything. The big bay windows looking out to sea, and what a view that was! For most certainly the Cornish coast is quite the most marvellous we have. The carpet was soft to the feet, the bed comfortable; she did not dare to lie down for a short rest, she said afterwards, because she knew that she would fall asleep, and heaven only knew when she would wake up. There was a bathroom attached. One can imagine the thrill of that after having a nurse's room in a big hospital, and queuing up for baths (and often having to come away because there just was not the time to wait).

'I have *not* made a mistake,' she told herself,

'I have done the wisest thing of all my life, and I have stepped out of the other world into sheer heaven.'

It seemed like that—then.

*   *   *

She changed for dinner, for Janet the housekeeper came up to see her and suggested this. Apparently Miss Sutcliffe adhered to this sort of thing and preferred it. Then Janet sent for the very nice little maid by the name of Fanny, who said it was her job to attend to visitors, and see that they had everything they could possibly want.

Bridget selected a lime-coloured dress with a loose silken fringe round the hem and the sleeves. She would feel better when she had actually met her patient, who she gathered was already feeling more herself, and they would meet after dinner.

'Mr. Clare will help you if there is anything you are wanting,' Janet said.

'He has already been most kind.'

'Yes, Nurse. He is Miss Sutcliffe's adopted nephew, and she is ever so fond of him. She has been very lonely, poor lady, all her own people dead, and no real friends to turn to.'

'I see.'

'Save, of course, Mr. Alan Thane from the farm. He is ever so good to her. He has such a lot of books, and brings armfuls of them for her to read, which is a big help.'

'I met him on the train coming down.'

'Did you now, miss? Nurse, I mean.' Janet was one of those women who was never going to be caught out at anything. She was kind, indeed very kind in all ways, and she was extremely pleasant.

'He travelled with me, and told me about his library. He must be a very clever man.'

'Oh he is, miss, ever so clever! One of the richest farmers in this part of the world, so they do say. You'll be seeing a lot of him, for he comes round here most days. Miss Sutcliffe is a very quick reader.'

'I see.'

Bridget finished dressing when she was left alone, and wondered if every night would mean a long chat with this old woman, and if so, how would she bear it? Glancing in the long mirror, she knew that she looked very nice indeed. The lime-coloured dress suited her, and it is wonderful how one can become transformed. She had overcome her worst tiredness, had stretched her limbs and got away from the limitations of a railway carriage, which on a distance of this length can be extremely palling.

Beyond the windows lay the sea, and she gloried in it. 'I *am* glad that I came,' she told herself yet again.

She opened the door, and went downstairs.

At this moment she had the feeling that she was stepping out into a new world; her whole life had changed, and everything about it. She was living against a background of a kind which she had never known before.

Janet, who was a darling, had told her that she should go down the stairs, turn left, and the first door she came to would be what they called 'the little room', a sort of ante-room to the dining-room where they had dinner. The stairs were magnificent, they gave you the idea of gliding down some shallow runway (they were so *un*steep), and at the bottom she turned into the 'little room'. It was smaller than she would have expected in such a big house, the furniture covered with a rose-patterned chintz, and long french windows opened out on to the rose garden, just coming into full glory with summer. It was a stiff, formal garden, a square, with a pool in the centre and on it superb white water lilies in flower. The paved paths split around the four beds, one at each corner, edged now with white pinks whose scent was overwhelming, and blooming with pink roses and madonna lilies. She thought that she had never before seen anything quite so beautiful. The garden was backed by a clipped yew hedge, orthodox and in perfect order. They must keep a hundred gardeners here, she thought.

The little room, with its vividly rose-patterned chintz everywhere, carried out the aura of charm. Undoubtedly, Gay Sutcliffe adored her home, and did her best to make it truly lovely.

Julian was already there. He was standing in the window. He wore a light dinner jacket, of silk she imagined, the colour of putty, and it struck her as being very elegant. He gave the impression of being a very rich young man as he spoke to her.

'So you got down here safely? It is a difficult house in which to find your way, but a happy house, in spite of its gloomy associations with the wreckers.'

She said, 'I'm ignorant. What did the wreckers *do?*'

He laughed. 'They were Cornish folk of all sorts, fishermen usually, who wished to fish more widely, smuggle more easily, and get away with it. Big ships came past carrying luxuries such as brandy, wines, tobacco. The men knew every inch of the coast and when the hour came they changed the lights, the navigation marks and such, and some wretched ship floundered on to the rocks, and then the wreckers looted it.'

'But what sort of men were they?'

'Just outsiders in a big way. They killed instantly. This is a rough part of the coast, and many drowned with a knife in their backs; some got away, but precious few, I warrant. Oh, the wreckers had a very bad name, which has gone on living after them, and they deserved it every

64

time.'

'I'm sure they did,' and then, 'are there any of them still alive? Or is that all over?'

'The smuggling is never over,' and he laughed at the thought. 'Every bit of this sea has its own secrets, as you may guess. Quite a lot of contraband comes sneaking into this part of the world. It is fairly easy to pick up most things that you want. They don't call themselves wreckers these days, and I doubt if men are murdered. We have got a bit more reasonable about such things, but misadventures do occur!'

'I hope there are none whilst I am here!'

'Wrong time of the year. This is not the time for high seas and mighty gales. Look out there. The sea is so clear and so blue that you would never believe that it could do more than murmur. But this *is* a hard sea, it rises in a moment, and kills on the instant. I would never trust the sea.'

Then he changed the subject. He spoke of his adoptive aunt and what a darling she was. 'I want to see her,' Bridget said.

'And you shall, the moment we have dined. She has hers upstairs, likes it better that way, unless it is one of her very good days, and she has wonderful days at times. When God is good.' He gave a laugh. 'God is not always so very good, I must say.'

'Tell me about her. How did you meet her?' she asked.

He was abroad in the mountains beyond Innsbrück, and he said they were quite the most wonderful mountains in all the world. He went out for a walk, and Gay—who was staying at the same hotel—had done exactly the same thing. She was one of those people who adore beautiful views, are wildly inquisitive, and desperately want to know more about people and places. 'I suppose every writer feels this way, because he seeks to write books, and life itself offers the best plots.'

But she had gone too far, was lost in a lonely field, and he found her and brought her home. She was a woman who was always very grateful for help, and they became friends. He drove her wherever she wished to go, in his car. She liked to be taken to some spot about which she wished to write, and then be left alone there for a bit with a notebook, so that she could collect material for her book. He understood her; they got on well together, and in the end he had managed to persuade her out of a desperate terror of flying, and bring her home this way.

The friendship had not died on that one holiday.

It was at the time when she was buying this house, and was full of ideas for improvements; he had introduced her to an architect friend of his who had the most amazing ideas of his own; all three of them had spent hours on the matter, and the house was the result.

'It's just lovely.'

'We adore it. I spend as much time down here with Gay as I can, for she looks on me as an adopted nephew. She ought to have married, of course, that was a shame.'

'Yes.'

'The one man in her life died in the last few days of the Second World War, and she says he was the only man she ever truly cared for. He died, and she pledged herself never to look at any other man. Gay is like that. She gets strange ideas, and does she abide by them!'

It was one of those perfect dinners which make your mouth water, for Janet was a superb cook. Julian declared that there was nothing she could not make, and always made it well.

They had iced soup, followed by fillets of sole served with gooseberries, which Bridget had never tasted before. There were lamb cutlets, with a sauce which she could not quite place, but which was delicious. An iced pudding, and a cheese soufflé.

'Now we go upstairs for coffee,' he said.

'This is where I get cold feet!'

'You needn't. You are about to see the nicest woman in all the world, I can promise you that.'

They went up the shallow stairs, which never gave one the idea of climbing at any time, along the corridor, then turned to a suite of rooms with double doors to them. Entering the first, one saw that it was a very charming sitting-room, exquisitely furnished, and with the most delightful pictures in it. At one time when her hands were more obedient to her wishes, Gay had done a lot of sketching, it was that which had originally brought her down to this part of the world.

The double doors led to the rest of the suite, a passage with bathroom to one side, a dressing-room on the other, and at the far end the big bedroom. This was a room with windows all round it, and from each you could see the sea. Tonight it was a calm, pale green-blue with little waves breaking below them. She had never realized how on this part of a very dangerous coast the sea could seem so bright; later the circling beams from the lighthouse would light up the passing ships at sea. The view from the windows was quite superb.

The room was soft blue, a blue which in some lights could have been a pale green. A door led into an ornate bathroom, and there was a tiny kitchenette on the other side, where, so Janet had told her, cups of tea could be made quickly and small things cooked, as the patient wanted them. A huge desk stood in one window, mahogany, that richly warm wood which always has a glow on it. The air was of luxury, no shortness of money here, but an air of calm and of peace, something which perhaps every author wants more than he dares say.

The woman herself was very pretty. Her hair

had not greyed, nor was it dyed. It was light, fair hair, curling at the ends, and enchanting. She had eyes which were the colour of the true bluebells of Scotland, which one sees everywhere in August. She was flushed and it struck Bridget that she also was a trifle worried about things; after all, meeting a new nurse, and not being at all sure that you will like her, *is* a tricky job! Pink and white, she had a radiant smile, and sat there wrapped in a light heliotrope dressing-gown, the colour of the flower itself.

'So you've got here, Nurse, oh, I am so glad!'

'I had a lovely journey down here.'

'I am sure you did. It is one of those days when this part of the world is playing up, and being its best.'

'It is far lovelier than I ever thought.'

'I found that, also. I came here and fell in love with it, and have been here ever since.' She indicated the chair nearest to her. 'Have you ever met an author before, or aren't you "booky"?'

'I've never met one before.'

Gay laughed, and she had a charming little voice, as if she thought life the greatest fun. 'The only difference between us and everybody else is that we see stories in everything. We are a little mad, but I hope you will learn to excuse that. Please? Now I have been stricken with this wretched complaint.'

'You've got a good doctor?'

'I had a dear, one of my reasons for coming to live here, but he went abroad two years back, and now we have another man, ex-R.N. His name is Hubert Forbes, and I think he is a very good doctor, though a little bit plain-spoken at times. I am sure he means well, and he and Julian spend days out fishing together. But I like him and he is very kind to me.'

'I'm glad. It makes all the difference in the world if one likes one's doctor.'

'But nothing and no one can cure me. I know this.'

'I should not be so sure.'

Gay lifted her head, and for a single moment gave Bridget a searching look, which seemed to go right through her. She said, 'You're a nice girl, but don't buoy me up with false promises.'

'There are new things being tested right now. My own hospital is making tremendous advances in their experiments.'

'Your own hospital, the one where Frank Dene trained, is experimenting?'

'Yes, it is.'

Bridget knew that her patient was enormously pleased. A flash of hope had shot through her world, and how she needed it! Miss Sutcliffe had been extremely beautiful; she had retained those sparkling blue eyes, and a ravishing smile. She told the story of how she had been suddenly crippled by her illness. One day she had been a

70

quite ordinary person going about the daily chores, and next day had awakened to find that her body had become stiff, that she could hardly move, and was in considerable pain all the time.

It had come on as suddenly as that.

One day herself, effervescent and passionately fond of long walks, driving a car, and bathing, then in an instant completely crippled. She had never been entirely out of pain since.

'Whom have you consulted?' Bridget asked.

'Everybody. Not just the Harley Street tribe, but the Germans who are better with this trouble than any of our men. I kept on telling myself that one of these mornings I should wake without it, and the pain would have gone just as it had come. But it has never happened.'

'It has been exactly the same ever since that first frightful morning when you found you had got it?'

'Yes, exactly.' She paused, then she went on again. 'In a way, I have become used to it. I have good and bad days, they come and go. One always prays that tomorrow will be better. I so wanted today to be a good one, for your sake, for I felt that Fate brought you to me,' and she laughed gaily enough. She had this tremendous faculty of being happy about life, yet must be in pain. Bridget had never thought that she would be so nice, or such a charmer, in spite of the things that she had read about her in the newspapers.

The coffee was brought up and set before them. Good coffee in little cups which were peach-coloured with a single rose on the side of each, a rose most beautifully painted. It was Julian who spoke.

'Gay hates talking about her malady, and she loves people and things; she wants to know what is going on in the world, and what she will do next. You come from London, don't you?'

'A long time training in a London hospital does not give a lot of time to know about people and things,' Bridget said.

'But it was fun?' Gay asked.

'Not always! When Matron knew that I was coming down here it was anything but fun; she was furious and wanted me to go back on it. Most girls go into the wards and start their work there, doing two years. I wanted a breather.'

'I should think you did!' Gay Sutcliffe laughed again, and she had the most entrancing laugh. 'Come and investigate Cornwall. Here we have ghoulies and ghosties, and things that go bump in the night. They won't ever hurt you if you take them in your stride; I'll show you the way.'

It was a delicious room, with the most beautiful pictures of the Lake District on the walls. Apparently before poor Gay was so afflicted she had been a very excellent artist. Bridget had always wanted to visit the Lake District and had read every book that she could get on Coniston 'Old Man', and Wastwater, and the little chapel there for the climbers who fell to their deaths. Gay had herself adored that part of the world, but knew that she would never be able to stand the winters there, and for that reason had kept clear. Down here it was warmer for her, but she always had a nostalgic hunger for the Lakes, and only prayed that one day she would recover and be able to go back there, and she smiled as she said so.

'I loved Old Man,' she said, 'and Scafell. It would be heaven to go back, and deep down inside me there is a strange superstitious feeling which tells me one-day-perhaps. Maybe all of us see life that way—One-day-perhaps.'

They talked of Bridget's early convent training, and Gay deprecated the ghastliness of the meals and the way in which they were served. Convents were all very well, she said, and undoubtedly they brought you up to be a good girl, and made you into a *very* good girl, but my goodness! there were a lot of things from which you wished to escape.

Gay was a Catholic, too, and somehow Bridget felt that this was a bond between them, and she would get somewhere.

'I hope you had a good dinner tonight,' Gay said.

She told the truth. 'The best I have ever had!'

Gay flung back her head and laughed; she was a very spontaneous person, one to whom you

73

could talk for ever. She said, 'I was your age once. I know I don't look like it, but I was, and I was brought up in a convent. They are kind, they do you well, but I always felt they did my mother a great deal better. Those sago puds, that eternal hash and stew, day in, day out.'

'I do know,' she agreed.

'I hate eating to plan. I have a list of the rules in my house. No milk puds with all that beastly skin on them; no stewed apple or rhubarb. I was brought up on that at home, and I want no more of it *ever*.'

She meant it, too.

Because the women seemed to be getting on so well, and he was only in the way, Julian slipped downstairs to find the doctor. They had planned to fix up another day's fishing in the morning, and the peaceful sunset looked to be the right auspice for that, foreshadowing good weather.

Gay and Bridget talked. They spoke of the specialists whom she had consulted, the two big operations she had had, and from which she had derived no benefit at all. She had reached the stage when medicine made her nervous.

She said, 'You may think me a silly old fool (as we grow older, we grow sillier, of course), but I am ever praying that one day some new discovery will be made, and I shall go skipping about and enjoying myself yet again.'

'Keep that hope warm within you,' Bridget

advised, 'for there is a destiny which shapes our ends. Nothing is impossible, whatever the doctors say. Refuse to be depressed, and cling to hope, for this is the world's best medicine.'

'You're a dear thing,' her new patient said with the sound of a sob in her voice. And then, 'Of course, given time, they will get a cure, that I know, and am just praying that I live long enough.'

'You will, I get hunches,' then she changed the subject. 'I met such a charming man in the train today coming down here. A Cornishman, too. He knows you and lives nearby, for he showed me the house.'

'It must have been Alan Thane. A wonderful man. His people farmed that land in the eighteenth century, and he still does. His hobby is a library and he lets me take what I will from it. I am a great reader. You'll very soon learn the way to and fro to his house, and fetch me fresh books.'

'You read yourself to sleep?'

'I try to. No, there is nothing to worry you in this. Not for the world would I ever keep you awake just because I was in pain, or could not sleep. You . . . you like to go to bed early?'

Bridget smiled. 'We do not get the chance in hospital. If you are on duty you come off at six or eleven, and I got a lot of the eleven touch. I don't know why, but I did.'

'And then went straight to bed in a little dog-hole of a room, I'm sure?'

'It was a little dog-hole all right, but I didn't go to bed. The place was fairly quiet then, and I could learn off strings of those awful Latin names for drugs. I was particularly stupid at them, and was for ever slogging away.'

'You poor thing! All over now?'

'I pray so.'

Gay paused. 'I cannot think why girls take it up. The food is awful, the rooms mere dog-holes, and the hours stupendous, yet every year thousands of girls work to qualify, and then perhaps get outside jobs which are even worse.'

Looking at her, Bridget thought that she seemed tired. 'You ought to be getting to sleep. Let me help a bit?' she suggested.

'I read in bed.'

'All right, let me get it all fixed for you?'

'I don't want to work you to death, and really there is nothing for you to do tonight. You'll find little Fanny will help you; she is a very nice girl, a fisherman's daughter. He went down when we lost the lifeboat ten years back, you possibly remember that? But lifeboatmen still go out and risk their lives, and here they think nothing of it. My goodness, they *have* got courage!'

'And I want to help you, just a wee bit, to bed. Let me fetch the hot water bottle?'

'All right.'

In the little kitchenette, where there was a

cupboard which had everything in it, she found the kettle and put it on to boil. Whoever had worked here before her, had been orderly, and prepared to do everything she could. She filled the bottle, got it into the bed, and was then surprised that Gay actually let her help her on to the bed. That, she knew, was a big step forward.

'You see, I do want to earn my money,' Bridget told her.

'I do understand, you will help me, and if at any time I can help you, Nurse, turn to me, do.'

She got down the satin dressing-gown and lovely nightdress. The curtains of the window were drawn back, and they could see the lights at sea, the ships continually coming and going, and a famous lighthouse on the horizon.

'You must love all this?' Bridget said.

'Some fear the sea, but I love it,' Gay replied gently, 'also those who work on it. This is the only place where I want to live, and die, and then rest for ever.'

CHAPTER FOUR

When finished, Bridget went to her room, a bell-push between herself and the patient, yet she knew it would never be used unless Gay was really ill. She was not one of those women who enjoy bad health; her malady crippled her cruelly, it was inescapable and dire, and Bridget felt for her. She had seen too many of these agonizing cases. There was, of course, a new drug; in the last six months she had found herself continually interested in its progress. But it all took time. For the moment the powers-that-be did not trust it far, but she felt that anything which could help at all, was worth trying.

In her comfortable bedroom everything was well arranged, and, as Bridget knew, she should be very happy here and content. She got into bed. The room was beautifully planned, and quite the best that she had ever slept in, and for a while she sat in bed by the window, with the heavy curtains pulled back so that she could sit and from here could see the ships gliding to and fro. The air was fresh and sweet, the sea calm. She had been lucky to come here, she told herself, and not for the world would she have gone back to the hospital. As she watched, she heard the sudden sound of a shot. It spat up into the air. 'Whatever could that be?' she asked herself, but she was sure that on such a calm night it could not be the lifeboat. Yet she was wrong. Within a matter of minutes another shot spat up into the night; soon she was to learn that this was the signal to warn the ship in distress that the lifeboat had started for them and was on its way. She saw it moving fast, plunging

78

through the sea, setting out on its quest. She waited for a time, believing that in such a calm sea there could be nothing wrong. Then she dozed off. Long afterwards she heard the gun which told her that the returning lifeboat had been sighted and would be back in a few moments.

She went to sleep again.

She woke early, dressed, and went downstairs not quite sure of what she was supposed to do. In the small dining-room a lavish breakfast was spread on the table, and Julian Clare was already there.

'So here we are again!' said he, 'I hope you had a good night in spite of the lifeboat setting out in the middle of it all.'

'Did they save any lives?'

'I don't know about that. I hear it was a couple of Borstal boys who pinched a boat further along the coast, and thought any fool could manage it. They had not got very far before the coastguards noticed that there was something funny afoot, then discovered what it was; a boat had been reported missing, and out went the lifeboat. I imagine that when they got the two lads they made them go through merry hell; and serve them right!'

'Did they think they would escape?'

'Probably, but it was a silly thing to try, especially with this coast, which is not the easiest in England.'

Bridget paused for a moment. 'Do you think I ought to go and see my patient first of all?'

'She hates being disturbed. Loves to be independent when she can. If Gay wants anything, then she will ask me, and I will pass it on to you. I shouldn't worry myself too much. She likes to ring when she wants help. She hates strangers butting in; that's the way she puts it. I give her most of her medicines. She likes me to be about the place. I warn you that she can be difficult, very difficult, but she is the most wonderful woman at heart.'

She looked at him with a faint suspicion of doubt in her mind. She had thought him so utterly charming when they had first met, but now, for some absurd reason, she was not quite sure.

She said, 'But whatever happens, I have to know what medicines she is taking. I understand that the doctor comes over every day. He will be here to instruct me this morning.'

Julian Clare laughed. 'That's it! His name is Hubert Forbes and he was in the Navy during the war, helping them along! Then he came here. It is not much of a village really, quite a small place, not the sort where you would have expected him to settle for ever, but he is mad keen on fishing and spends most of his life at it, often with me. He puts fishing before medicine, I'd say. He lets Gay do whatever she wishes, poor lamb, and he knows that there is precious little more can be done to help her. But he is kind and that is what matters.'

Bridget did not know what to say; she was too new to the patient to be able to give an opinion, and nervous as well. She did not like the thought of Julian Clare giving her medicines, when she did not know what they were. He went on talking.

'This is your first outside job, isn't it? You're lucky it's easy, and she is such a dear amiable creature, such a charmer. I'll always help you,' and he smiled at her. She had to admit that he had the most ravishing smile that she had ever seen.

After breakfast was done she went up to see how her patient was getting on. She prayed she would be told the truth, but already had found that Gay liked to make light of her troubles.

She went into the little ante-room beautifully tidied, for there were maids about the place who could do this well, and she went into the bedroom. The patient was sitting up in bed surrounded by fresh frilled pillows. She confessed to a bad night, which her eyes gave away before she even mentioned it, and she had not wanted her breakfast by the look of things, for the tray was scarcely touched, just a half-emptied coffee cup, and one of the pretty patterned plates had some toast left on it.

Bridget pretended to notice nothing, which

was always half the art of making oneself popular, as she knew. For the moment she must hold back. As yet she had had too little experience of private nursing to risk any mistakes, and she had been highly suspicious of the remarks that Julian Clare had made. The medicines were on the far table; she eyed them with doubt. Two she recognized as being something of which she was sure; a third bottle was nameless, and she could not place it; there were also some small twists of paper which she did not understand. But whatever she did, she must take her time. Her work here was to help the patient; to defend the patient, and to work for her.

She said, 'Now what about your medicines? You'll have to guide me, as yet.'

'I've had the early morning ones.' Miss Sutcliffe was looking utterly worn-out, as if she had hardly had a minute's sleep. 'Julian is such a dear boy, and does everything for me. He brings my medicine to me first thing. Somehow he always seems to know when I have had a bad night. I think the lifeboat going out always disturbs me, then I can't get to sleep again.'

'How about something soothing right now?' Bridget suggested.

'Oh, I . . . I wouldn't know.'

She was restless, poor thing, tired out, of course, and sad at heart. Anyone suffering from an incurable disease must get wearied and sad however much one tried to help. This was not the moment to remonstrate, but it was the moment to watch her patient closely, and try to find out a little more about her. Apparently the doctor was going out for a long day's fishing today; he would pop in fairly early, just to see how she was, before he started, and he actually arrived much sooner than Bridget had expected.

He was a stocky, little man, about fifty years of age, she thought, with very dark, very vivid eyes, and instinctively she felt that he hated disclosing his feelings. He was a man who seemed as if he stood behind the fireproof curtain in a theatre. It was impossible to touch him. Impossible to ascertain what it was he really meant or wanted. He had retired from the Navy, where he had achieved little. In the Service bad cases were shipped ashore to the men who could really cope with them, and the very ordinary cases were all that one could hope to treat on board. These were very limited in their scope.

Dr. Forbes said, 'Hello, Nurse!' and to the patient, 'Hello, m'dear, how's things? Not one of our better mornings, I see, but tomorrow is always another day,' and he tittered. Instantly he had stamped himself as being the sort of doctor Bridget could never really like.

He said to her, 'I'm early, not unusual for me, but I'm having a day's fishing, so have to be on time with Julian.'

'So he told me.'

Quite plainly the doctor and his patient were on the best possible terms, for poor Gay Sutcliffe honestly believed that he was doing his best for her, and she trusted him completely. He soothed her, flattered her quite a lot, and teased her a little. She appeared to like it. Then he said good-bye.

'Just a word with you, Nurse,' he said.

'Yes, Doctor?'

They were outside the door and standing in the ante-room where she faced him. He was all for hurrying through the interview, plainly not caring for it too much. 'I'm afraid, poor little soul, that she is in a pretty bad way, and there is not very much that we can do, as you know. Keep her happy. Keep her amused. Enjoy the good days and try to get her comfortably through the bad ones.'

'Yes, Doctor.' Then, 'She is taking nothing more than the medicines on the table?'

'No, those are all there are for the moment. Our backroom boys have not got very far with this complaint, though they have been trying for years, but there you are.'

She said, but cautiously, for she knew that this could be difficult, 'We have been very fortunate recently at my own hospital with the new drug, Encildin. Possibly you do not like it?'

Instantly his eyes challenged hers, and she recognized it as a challenge. He would not stand any interference, that was plain, he intended to say what he had to say. His lips curled slightly at the corners, and he said, 'Yes, I know. It is one of the new fads which are for ever coming up, and they go as quickly as they come. We both know that for the moment there is no cure for this poor lady, try as we will. Nothing more can be done for her than is being done at this very moment. We have to try to keep her happy, interested in outside matters and able to talk, and that sort of thing. Today is a bad one. Such days are a bit too frequent, and it would *have* to happen on your first day here.'

She nodded. 'I have nursed these cases, Doctor, and it is a malady which brings too many bad days with it, alas.'

'That's it! Well, I must get away for my fishing. Wish me luck. I leave you in charge here, for Julian is coming with me. Just pander to her, spoil her, make her as happy as you can,' and he moved to the door. It was quite obvious that he had no intention of holding on for a single moment longer than was necessary.

Bridget would never know why she spoke her own mind, but she did. She said, 'There are other cures that could be tried. It is not right that there is nothing that can be done, for we have had some quite startling effects in hospital. Has she run the gamut?'

She felt him going cold with anger. A trifle impatiently he said, 'You really must trust us to try everything that we possibly can, because it is for her future. And when I say we *have* tried everything, I mean everything, not just picking and choosing this one and that one. Please understand this. When I say we have tried everything, then I *mean* everything.'

He walked out of the room, and she knew that she had made a bitter enemy for herself, and was annoyed. She should have held her tongue, but she felt strongly about this case. She knew that this form of arthritis was said to be incurable, but, given time, all diseases *are* curable; one day we should have the answer to cancer.

She said, as he went, 'Unhappily this sort of case gets too many bad days. I wish one could help more.'

From the doorway he said, 'You must trust me to know best. I qualified as a doctor. You are a nurse. Nurses *obey* orders,' and he shut the door behind him. She knew that she had made a bad mistake, and worst of all, Gay Sutcliffe swore by this doctor. She turned again to the patient.

She was glowing over her doctor; she adored him. 'I am sure that you found him quite wonderful, Nurse,' she said. 'He is a real charmer, and has worked wonders for me.'

'I am sure he has.'

'He has had a difficult life. He married the wrong girl and they parted within a year. Then he hated being in the Navy, sheer hard work, and all the interesting cases packed ashore to hospital, and he got left with just the headaches, the backaches and the toothaches. He retired because he could not bear it. I thank God every day for the fact that we have such a good man here in the neighbourhood. I owe everything to him.'

'Yes, I am sure,' and all the time she felt this doubt within herself; the terror that this man was not to be trusted. She thought that somehow his friendship with Julian Clare was curious. One would have thought that they had nothing in common, save love of fishing, yet she should not feel this way, it was no business of hers anyway. She did not want to talk about him, because privately she felt badly about him. She went on tidying up the room, and drew back the flowery curtains. There beyond them lay the sea so blue that it might have been a noble string of aquamarines hung about the very throat of England itself.

She went downstairs, for the secretary would be coming up to talk to her patient, and this was the hour in the morning when they were left alone together and the writing began. She meant to go across to Alan Thane's farm, for there was a book which Miss Sutcliffe had finished, and Miss Sutcliffe was always nervous of anything happening to them if they were left lying about. She told Janet where she was going.

'You'll be taking Smutty with you, won't you,

Nurse?'

'If you think the dog will come with me?'

'Oh, he loves a walk, he will go with anybody. He gets too few walks, poor wee mannie!'

The moment she called him, Smutty, a small Scottie, came galloping up. They set off together, and it was a lovely day. Now she could see the marvellous view which lay before her, the glorious shadow of clouds beating their way across the sky, and reflected here on the big expanse of fields. This was wondrous country, with here and there clusters of pine trees growing together. She could see in the distance the strange outline of hills, miles away. This was the far end of England, but a mile or so from Land's End itself, where every day motor coaches went in their dozens.

Smutty thought it magnificent.

They turned from the road, down the narrow lane which led to the farm. The hedges were rather stunted, but wild roses blossomed in their amiable pink. There was the last of the tall campions and the big marguerites. It was a flowery countryside, and everywhere there was the cotton grass which fascinated her, for she had never seen it before.

She could see the farm in far more detail, and it was larger than she had thought. There was a group of compact barns to one side, beautifully thatched; and then there was the farmhouse with its slate roof, everywhere there seemed to be slate roofs, and before it a formal garden. It was a very beautiful garden, and entirely unexpected. There was a long pergola leading to the front door, with the big veranda beyond. The garden was grassy with a formal lily pool cut square, the way she liked it best, and with pale pink and white lilies in blossom on it. There were irises also; she went to the front door and rang the bell. A manservant answered it, the man whom she knew as being Dick. He took her inside.

'If you would please sit down, miss? Mr. Thane will be back in a moment and I will bring in some coffee.'

She sat down.

The veranda was not a conservatory, but actually another sitting-room. The thick green carpet gave the appearance of moss, and climbing plants grew up the walls, under the glass roof. A plumbago had serene blue blossom. Surely the most exquisite blue in all the world? Some white roses, with a superb scent. On the table at the far end there were all manner of growing flowers. It was a room one would have loved to sit in, bright with sunshine, refreshingly warm, and cut off from the wind. Already she had to learn that the Cornish wind was something strong.

Dick returned with a comfortable-looking tray of coffee. The cups were Royal Worcester china, and she noticed this as he set it down beside her. There were little iced biscuits which tempted her, and some small home-made rock cakes.

'Mr. Thane won't be long, miss,' he said, 'and he would wish you to start, I am sure.'

'I ought to wait for him.'

'It will only get cold, and he wouldn't like that.'

So she did help herself, and was glad that she had done it, for Alan was some time. When he came in, he was wearing farming gear, a pair of cord breeches, and gum boots. The dark red cotton shirt was open at the chest, and short above the elbows. He had well-brushed hair, for he was a very tidy man, and bright, laughing eyes. He was one of those men who always manage to convey their personality, by the way they look, by their amiable laugh, and instinctively she knew that she liked him enormously. He was a man who could make one very happy.

'I am so sorry. You have been waiting here for ages, but I got stuck. Trouble with one of my best cows, but it is all over now, and we have got the loveliest little bull calf you ever saw.' He spoke about it with an immense satisfaction, almost as if the calf were his own child. 'You've got some coffee? Good! Dick is a decent lad in that way, and can always be trusted to look after a visitor properly for me. I suppose Gay sent you back with the book? I've got another here, that I

90

promised her, and it is one she very much wants to read. Could you take it back with you?'

'But of course I could.'

He picked it up, a first edition carefully wrapped in cellophane, so that it should not be scarred in any way.

'Gay is a charmer,' he said. 'It is such a shame that she should be afflicted with this infernal arthritis. What a menace it is, and far too many have it these days. It's high time your lot found out the answer, I should have said.' Then he paused. 'What about Julian? How do you get on with him? He is a strange nut to crack.'

'Oh, we get on all right. He has been very kind in promising to take me out and show me places. I feel in some ways that he is inclined to take a bit too much on to himself. He wants to be in charge of the medicines, and give her everything himself, which is not right.'

'Of course it isn't!' He looked very directly at her, as if he was trying to read further down into her heart. 'You'll have to arrange matters better than that, and show him where he gets off.'

'Yes, of course, but I am not at all sure that he is the sort of fellow who does get off,' and she shrugged her shoulders. 'Miss Sutcliffe is a real darling, and I feel deeply sorry for her, and only wish that I could be of real help to her.'

Alan looked at her more closely.

He said, 'My dear, you are the one who *is* going to help her in the long run, I know that. I felt that when we travelled down here together. Be good to her, for she is really a very sweet personality, and we are all so fond of her. You see, I am not quite so sure that the house is truly lucky for her. I know she thinks it is, but is it? Her doctor is a darned good fisherman, but I should hate to trust my life to him, for I should not think that he knew that much. Too many people come here for the fishing, for the good air, for the actual life of the sea.' He lit a cigarette, she thought a trifle nervously. 'There are so many things that I feel ought to be done for her; I'm deeply interested in her case, and so much want to help her.'

'So do I,' she interrupted quickly.

He glanced at her. 'You and I have got into this difficult affair,' he said, 'I feel, to help each other out of it all, for it *is* a worry. I wish I knew sufficient medicine; I know about it with animals, but that's not good enough.'

'It's nice to have someone here on my side,' she said.

At that moment she heard the voice of Smutty giving tongue, and looking through the window saw a large Buff Orpington hen in flight, making a terrible noise, and coming behind it full pelt, though not making much ground (for when chasing Smutty never bent his knees), the dog itself.

In an instant Alan was there.

He swept out of the front door, and

circumvented Smutty, who was coming straight at him. Nobody could say that Smutty was a clever dog. In a chase, he just chased, no more! One might guess that he shut his eyes, went as fast as he could, and hoped for the best!

'I'm sorry,' she said.

'In the country everyone knows that all dogs chase hens, which are silly birds anyway. Now if this had been a gander, it would have been Smutty coming to *us* in full flight!'

She laughed at the thought. Then she rose, the new book in her hand. 'High time I got back.'

'The doctor and Julian are out fishing?'

'Yes, it has to be an all-day job, I gather.'

'Probably.'

She said, 'Thank you for being so helpful and so kind, because I am very much alone here, and there will be times when I need help, as you can see.'

'Well, I'm here, I'm always here.' He walked to the gate with her, then put out a hand and laid it almost tenderly on her arm. 'You and I think alike about a lot of things, and that is to the good. If ever you find yourself in any worry, come round here and let me help you out of it, if I can. You can trust me. Remember this. I promise you that you can always trust me.'

CHAPTER FIVE

They had come to the gate which entered into
the garden, sprucely kept and quite beautiful.
One side the bigger gate led into the yards, and
there was a faint not unpleasant scent of
animals, a dark barn rising against the sky, the
sound of a cow lowing further away. For a single
moment Bridget stood there looking into this
man's eyes, not quite sure of herself, and feeling
as if for a single second she had been translated
into another world. Then she came to.

'I know that I can trust you, and that is quite
lovely,' was what she said.

'Things are strange at the Wreckers' House.
They always have been, and always will be, for
the thoughts that men once thought in a house
go on living there, they say. They are the eternal
tenants, I think. Maybe there is something of
the spirit that the wreckers left behind them.'

'Were they awful people? I am ashamed to
know so little, but they are rather beyond the
understanding of a person from the Midlands.'

'They were pretty dreadful. They lived by
their wits, of course, and did not care to what
limits those wits were stretched. They changed
the lights so ships were misled, they organized
wrecks, and drowned some of the men; a few
odd drownings were no worry to them. But

don't let's talk of it. I must pick you some flowers for Gay, I won't be half a minute.'

She watched him as he gathered the white roses and the loveliest of the delphiniums, so abundantly blue. It was a glorious garden; she did not wonder that he was proud of it. He was a man who adored reading, and had practically educated himself entirely this way.

He said, 'When I was a kid, I had a groggy ankle, which let me down. I suppose all of us get some little things that try us, it can't be helped, this is life. So I took up reading as a hobby, and reading is a magnificent education. Leastways to me.'

She took the flowers into her arms, and called Smutty, still hoping for another hen to chase. Poor little dog! He got very few walks according to Alan, who was a most understanding man, even when they were his own hens that were being chased.

She walked back to find that Miss Sutcliffe had now finished with her secretary, and was sitting there doing nothing. She was enchanted by the flowers, and the book was one which she specially wanted to read. Alan had a remarkably good taste in books, she told Bridget, and you could always rely on his choice.

The girl sat down beside her. She told the story of Smutty and the hen. Apparently this always happened every time he went there, for he was an inveterate chaser of hens. Miss

Sutcliffe adored dogs, and before she had been afflicted this way, took hers for miles along the cliffs almost every day.

'Then I don't have to ask for leave to take him out?'

'Oh, never! He knows his way back, and everybody in the neighbourhood knows him, so you won't lose him. But don't take him towards Land's End. Too many people are about there and it gets me scared. This part is okay for him.'

'I'll remember that.'

Bridget changed the subject. She said, 'Have you written all your life?'

'Mostly all my life. I was about eight years old when I began, and wrote fairy stories for my dolls. I believed in dolls, of course, and made sure that one day they would wake up and become real people. I thought they were here under a spell. Wicked fairy stuff,' and she laughed.

'And they helped with the books?'

'Did they not! I always relied on my dolls to give me a hand whenever a plot started to be difficult. They do that at times.'

'I thought you got it all worked out before you started?'

'Yes, and no. Suddenly one gets what one thinks is a better idea, and there we are, right out of the running again! Have you ever thought of writing books?'

'Yes. Yes, I have. I have always wanted to

write.'

'Can you type?'

'After a fashion, yes I would not say that anyone would ever give me a job typing, they would never pay for what I can do.'

'And spell?'

'I think so.'

'That is a pity, for they say that no real writer can ever spell properly. I am one of them. If you want to write a book, and if it is in your blood, you should do so, this is the place to start it. I can always be a help, or try to be a help, as much as is possible.' She smiled, she really was the most encouraging woman that Bridget had ever met. 'Just think about it, and if you want to do it, come and ask me more. I should *love* to help.'

'Bless you,' said the girl.

The fishermen did not get back until tea time, one of those lavish teas, with all manner of delightful sandwiches and iced cakes, Parkin and Cornish clotted cream, which is served up with everything in that part of the world. It was a world so far from the hospital that Bridget wondered how she could ever quite understand it.

The fishermen had had a good day, and were enchanted with their catch. This meant that there would be fish tonight, fresh as it could be, and tasting wildly different from anything that one ate in London. Bridget was hoping to get a word in with the doctor before he left them, but he had hardly started his tea when he was called away to a 'midder' case, which probably meant the entire evening. Then her own patient had another lie-down, and she was alone with Julian.

He had come back in very high spirits, and said that the day's fishing had done him good. He did not refer to this morning's talk for a time, then to her surprise he spoke of it.

'I'm afraid I snapped a bit this morning. I am never really at my best at dawn, it could be a hangover from the night before, or that I am a bad riser. I've never asked myself which it is. It is a darned bad habit of mine, and I'm sorry.'

She said, 'Lots of people feel just that way first thing in the morning, you know.'

'All the same, it is damned bad manners. I shut you up. Forget what I said, I was just in a bad mood. You are the nurse here, I am just the looker-on. I did do a few months in hospital, but found it all too much for me. My goodness, they work a chap to death, and then if possible cut him up and have a peep at his inside! I hated it.'

She ignored that, then she said, 'One has to realize that one of these days the real cure will be found, and people won't be stuck like poor Miss Sutcliffe is.'

'You're well versed! You bet they teach their nurses well!' and he glanced at her. At the same time she knew though he had apologized, and had been quite charming about it, the conversation had got them no further. Nothing more had been said about her having the medicines under her own wing. Now he changed the tune. 'I pray that you won't be too utterly lonesome here, for Cornwall *is* a lonely county. But there are wonderful places for you to see, all round us, and I'd love to take you to them. St. Ives, Mousehole, Penzance, Land's End, and all that it means. Sennen Cove.'

They were, of course, just names to her, no more. 'I'd love them all,' she said, and only hoped that her tone of voice did not disclose her eagerness, and her longing to see them. Land's End, stretching out into the sea towards the sunset at evening, Sennen Cove with fishermen's homes along the water's edge, Mousehole, where there are artists everywhere, and St. Ives, a town of tiny streets and alleyways, of thousands of cats, so they said, and fishermen's nets for ever drying.

'I—I'd love to see it *all*,' she said again.

'Right! Look here, there is time and I could take you for a run before dinner. Gay will sleep for a couple of hours now, she always does. Come with me.' His dark eyes were twinkling; he held out his hands, beautifully made hands, like some great artist's; he was a very good-looking man, of course, and he had the gay manner which was so inviting.

'I oughtn't to do it.'

'Yes, you ought. You're going to do it, anyway.' He had her hand still in his, and was running with her down the stairs, and across the hall to where the car waited. 'Come and see Cornwall, and fall in love with a dream!' was what he said.

They went to the wishing-well on the hill, there to stake her claim on a first-class wish.

A group of fir trees surrounded it, etched against the skyline, and the locals vowed that here the piskies granted wishes. There was a rough road, little more than a cart track, and the well itself with the fir trees quiet and peaceful clustering together and hushed by the oncoming of the night. There were tuffets of heather in the grass, vividly pinky mauve, and scabious fluttering in the wind, the occasional marguerite, and then Bridget saw the well. It was smaller than she had anticipated, and completely round.

He gave directions. 'You throw a coin in and wish, and they say the wish is granted within the year if luck is good.' He was laughing as he said it, his bright eyes dancing and the wind ruffling his hair. He certainly had a quality of beauty which she admired.

'And do wishes come true?'

'They say so. Every Cornishman believes devoutly in it.'

She did what she was told, and threw down a coin which fell into the clear water, then sank amongst a load of others. She wished for happiness, and one day to write books as Gay

Sutcliffe did; she wished to meet and marry a man whom she loved; all the heartfelt wishes of a young girl who is standing on the threshold of life, with all ahead of her.

'I know they'll never come true, but wish them just the same,' she said.

'They do, I know. There is no other county quite like our Cornwall, remember that one. They say it is the last stronghold of the "little people", and sometimes I begin to believe that myself, for this part of the world can be so convincing.'

It was funny that at the very moment she thought of Frank Dene, the man who had originally mentioned Gay Sutcliffe to her. She thought of the staff dance, where everything had gone dead wrong, and the new dress had been completely and utterly wasted; of Edgar Thorn. The whole hospital had warned her against him, as being the heart-breaker-in-chief, the man there was no escaping, the extraordinary flirt, and she had thought that she would marry him.

Now she very much doubted if anyone would ever marry Edgar Thorn, because he was the sort of man who flirted his way through life, getting the best out of it. But how he had hurt her! How she had wept and how wretched she had been!

Frank Dene had been goodness itself to her in suggesting that, anyway for a time, she came right away from it all, for it could do her no good at all. She was glad that she had made the effort, and it had entailed some effort, more especially that 'morning after' in Matron's office, with Matron smelling a rat and trying to get the truth out of her. She hoped when all this was over, and she had taken a long breath and now could live again, she would be able to go back there. Changed, of course. Older. Maybe the coin in the fairy pool surrounded by the fir trees, would save the situation for her, and wishes would come true.

But I'm glad that I came here, she thought.

'You've never seen a wishing-well before?' he asked.

'Of course not! I thought they were an invention.'

'You mustn't say that sort of thing in Cornwall.'

'But that was what I thought.'

He flung back his head and laughed, his hair catching the reflection of the sunlight, and his eyes dancing. 'This is the last bit of England where dreams really do come true, so be prepared for anything to happen, and always the unexpected.'

'Do *you* believe that?'

He leant closer, and she could see the little brown flecks in the iris of his eyes. 'I never know. Half of me does, the other half knows that there can't be fairies, and mermaids waddling about the country, and that wishing never brings a dream true.' He took her wrist and held it firm. 'Were you wishing for a dark love or a fair? Tell me?'

She was horrified that, for a moment, she thought again of Edgar Thorn, the man who she had been so sure loved her. She certainly *had* loved him. Somehow she knew that he was a jilt, and she did not suppose that he had given her a second thought. She thought again of Frank Dene, the E.N.T. specialist, the man who had given her the world's best possible advice: 'Get away from it all for a bit. Go right away to pastures new, for they always have something better to offer!' Already they had done just this.

'You must have had hundreds of admirers in your hospital,' said Julian, as she didn't answer.

'One doesn't go to hospital to have love affairs,' she told him. 'One goes there to learn, and one learns the hard way, I can tell you, and *all* the time! The worry is that when you have done a day's work (and they have you up at dawn), you are so tired that you could not raise another finger whoever asked you.'

'Why did you do it? There must be hosts of easier jobs and ones where you get more fun. I should hate it.'

She did not know why she spoke the truth and in such a way, but somehow the truth was the only answer to it. 'Operations! Possibly it is because there is no other job which gives much tremendous rewards as nursing. I have seen men and women recover as though by a miracle, and it is an amazing sight.'

'But look at the financial side! You get about twenty pounds a year, relic of Queen Victoria pocket money, surely?'

'More than that, but money is not the greatest thing in the world. There are, I suppose, rewards of the heart, the sort of things that thrill you with such rapture that it is uplifting. I always remember one young man lying as if dead in my arms and we had tried everything to get him round. The last effort was a hypodermic when all hope had gone, then the sudden flicker of an eyelash, the first sound, that little stir which tells you that he is still alive. I think those are the really wonderful moments when nothing else in the world can or does matter.'

He stared at her.

'You have infected me with it. What you say is true, obviously, bless you,' and he went quiet. Then gently he said, 'We'll have to go back to the car, for the sun is setting.'

They went to the car, through grass spotted by the fat mauve scabious here and there, and behind them the fir trees stirring now in the faint wind of evening, and her wish lying there in the water waiting to come true.

This young man was being very kind to her. He was goodness itself to his adoptive aunt, comforting her when the pain was bad, or when she fretted over the wretchedness of her infirmity. Bridget wished there were some cure to which one could turn. She had gone silent, perhaps because she was thinking of the fairy story of penicillin which had worked such magic in the world. Somewhere, somehow (if only one knew where and how), there must be a cure like it for this terrible arthritis.

'A penny for your thoughts?' he said.

'I was thinking what a strangely unusual part of the world this is. The fairies and the piskies, and the wishes being granted; every corner is so beautiful.'

'I don't *really* believe in the piskies.'

'Are you quite sure?'

He laughed as she said it, for she had nailed him down to the point. 'You've got me there! I can't believe in them, but I am taking no risks with them. They know what they are doing, and some of their forebodings do come true. I've proved that.'

She changed the subject when he got into the car, and they started driving off together. She began talking to him about the new cures which were as yet in the embryo, but being tried out. There was one for arthritis which was for ever at the back of her mind, because it had so wildly interested her. They had been using it in some cases in hospital recently and felt there *was* something in it.

He said, 'Yes, I know, but the disappointment is too great when they don't work. One has to remember this. It isn't fair.'

'Yet one day they must find the answer.'

'Not by experimenting on Gay! I care for her too much to let outsiders have a bash at her, and that is what it would amount to. It would run the risk of far too much disappointment and regret. The doc is a friend of mine, and he feels the same way.'

'One day the cure will come.'

'Yes, of course.'

They had to go faster for they had already been too long and had gone much further than they had originally intended. Apparently Gay Sutcliffe liked her meals to be punctual, Julian told Bridget, and the only thing which really annoyed her was when she had to wait for her dinner. They rushed the last five miles, and when they got to the door Bridget jumped out almost before they had stopped, and made a dash upstairs. Thank goodness, being a nurse meant that she could change at express speed, and with never a stud out of place or a button undone. The sharp eyes of Sister would have spotted that, and it was what was known as 'carelessness', which got a girl into lasting trouble. She laughed to herself as she stripped off her linen coat and skirt, and rushed into the little silk dinner frock.

Then she went to her patient.

Poor Gay! She had been having a bad time. The bother was that once she went down the hill she seemed to continue to go down, and now Dr. Forbes was with her. Seeing her like this, Bridget was dismayed that she had left her.

'I ought not to have gone,' she said.

'How were you to know that the pain would come back? Usually once it starts to go, it goes. It did not work according to the book of the words today, alas.'

She looked wretched ill, worn out, and Bridget was really ashamed of herself for having gone out and left her.

'Is it better now?' she asked Gay.

'Yes, lots better, and now you go down and have your dinner. Come back afterwards and tell me what you saw, and what you did. Get them to send the coffee up here, and we will have it together. I am getting better all the time and that will do me good.'

The doctor had left them together. The bedroom, a truly beautiful room, with long windows to the ground, which looked out to sea (and what a view that was!), led into Gay's writing-room. It was lined with books, most of them in the most brilliant bindings. A welter of work was piled on the desk. Gay had not felt quite well enough to deal with her letters for the last two days, so she said. Bridget saw the doctor standing there pulling on a light grey overcoat.

'She'll be all right now,' was what he said.

Somehow Bridget wanted to ask *the* question yet again. Maybe she should have held back, their dinner was ready, and Miss Sutcliffe had asked them to come back to her the moment they were through, but this was something she had to ask now. Maybe she rushed it (she was one of those people). She spoke to the doctor.

'I was wondering, Doctor, how she would react to the new drug we have been trying out in hospital? We had some quite surprising results. I know it is in its infancy, but all the great cures have to start sometime, and I feel anything is better than nothing.'

He looked at her. He was a man who never disclosed his feelings by a single expression on his face. She wondered if he had had some catastrophe in his life which had left a mark which he could not erase.

Very coldly he said, 'I am afraid, Nurse, that you have got to realize that I prescribe for my own patients, and this is my duty, not yours. Naturally, I know about the latest discoveries and ventures, and there are good reasons why the one you talk of should *not* be brought into action here. Miss Sutcliffe is *my* patient, and because you have been here for but a few brief hours, you cannot possibly understand her constitution as I can.'

She felt completely awestruck.

For a moment she clutched at the small table beside her for support, because she thought she would faint from sheer horror. How had she ever talked herself into this mess? There was a small ashtray standing on the table with a light drift of ash lying in it. As she looked closer, the ash caught the shimmer of sharper light on it, and she saw that it had fallen on a discarded hypodermic needle. It gleamed for a single second, and there was something about it that arrested her attention. She did nothing. She knew that if she said anything at this moment she would finish herself entirely, and she went dead still.

It was when she saw him looking at her, that she spoke again.

'I'm sorry, I meant well. . . .' No more.

'Yes, of course.' He buttoned the light overcoat together, fumbling a little, and then moved towards the door. She would be thankful when he had gone. He said, 'Everything that it is possible to do is being done for the patient. That is that.'

'She has had an injection?'

He was angry, snapping sharply at her, almost as if he swore before he spoke. 'No, of course not! She had the one this morning, when you were here, and that was sufficient. It is wrong to increase the dosage at this stage, it could not possibly do any good. I should never do that.'

'I see.' Half of her wanted to ask 'But what about the used hypodermic needle lying in the ashtray?' but she saw that this man was not in the mood for enquiry. She must be careful, for anyway he was the doctor in charge. 'Oh dear, whatever do I do?' she asked herself as she opened the door for him with the usual polite farewell. 'Thank you very much for all you have done, Doctor. We shall see you in the morning?'

She knew that he was furiously angry; he was a difficult man, as she had known from the first, possibly one of those failures in the medical world who drift into some small town where they would hardly be noticed. It was a pity that he had come into contact with Miss Sutcliffe, for Bridget did not trust him, and was concerned for her patient.

She shut the door quietly on him, went back to Gay and comfortingly smoothed her pillows.

She said gently, 'I am going down to dinner now, and afterwards we will come up here and sit with you for a bit, if you think you can bear it. You may be better then.'

'Thank you, dear.' Gay put out a badly deformed hand, bent like some old broom which has been used too often. It was dreadful what this arthritis could do when it came to wrecking the human body. She said lovingly, 'Dear Bridget, I am so glad you came to me, dear. You are such a nice girl, and so kind, bless your heart.'

Acting on impulse, Bridget stooped down and kissed her. 'I am going to get you better,' she said, and she meant it. 'Whatever the others say, I am determined to get you well again. I promise you I shall try everything there is in the world.'

'You may have a big job!' and the patient smiled.

For a single moment they clung together, and the kind eyes of the sick woman looked at her with pain in them, yet a warmth and a tenderness which were very reassuring. 'She is all alone in the world, poor thing,' Bridget told herself. She hated the thought that she had this useless Dr. Forbes, and somehow or other she suspected him, and could not think why. The memory of that used needle worried her; it had had no right to be there. Someone was cheating her. It could be the doctor, but it could be Julian Clare, she did not trust him.

Only this morning Janet had been strangely outspoken about the adopted nephew. He had been annoyed because his newspaper had not arrived at the usual time, and she had resented this, and when he had gone she had been very open about him.

'It isn't for me to say,' she admitted, 'but Miss Sutcliffe is such a dear kind lady, it is a shame that she should be struck down this way, then be at *his* mercy. I want her well again, oh my God I do!' She became secretive, leaning forward with a very confidential voice, 'And if you asks me, Nurse, that there so-called nephew of hers ain't no good to her. No good at all. Ever since she changed her will and left him every bit—oh yes, he made her do that—he has turned queer with her, and I don't like it.'

Bridget was embarrassed, and did not know what to say; what could she do? She herself had very few kind feelings for this handsome young man, even if he had been kind to her, and helped her to see more of Cornwall than otherwise she would have done.

'I knows as how I hadn't ought to say nothing!' Janet was becoming more and more confidential, 'but I am downright worried to death about the whole thing, I am. I've been along of her for ages now, and she is like one of my own kind, I'm fond of her, I am really.'

One had to gloss over it. One thing was certain, Bridget knew that she could not accept confidences and truths from people like this old dear, and she was very much afraid that they *were* truths, about what was going on in the household. She went down to dinner.

It happened to be one of the extra special dinners which were done so beautifully in the Wreckers' House. Everything was of the best— avocado pear, and then an iced soup which tasted of cherries in some strange way of its own. Fish and chicken, and an iced sweet.

'How did you find Gay?' Julian asked her.

'Not too well, poor darling. I gather that she had another injection. I didn't know a thing about it, and I don't like it. I want to know exactly what is going on. She seemed very collapsed.'

'Did she say anything about it?' There was a strange inflexion in his voice, which she did not quite understand.

For a moment she played with the idea of telling him what had actually happened, then she had the faint feeling that he might be concerned with it. She evaded the direct reply. 'I thought she was getting better, and she wanted us to go up there and sit with her afterwards.'

Julian looked at her.

'Of course. She knows we shall go up.' She got the idea that he was trying to read right down into her heart. His eyes were clear and bright, and his mouth was half laughing. He said, 'I do advise you, my dear, don't try to keep things from me. I suppose I know most of the things that go on in the Wreckers' House, I ought to, anyway. Remember I am your friend. We've got to be friends, you and I.'

'I ... I'm keeping nothing from you,' she said, and her voice was quite firm.

Somehow she knew that this was not the truth. Somehow she felt here in this room something which she could not see, it could even be a ghost, something that the wreckers had left behind them. It was now, quite suddenly, that she realized how deeply she cared for her patient, and now she was aware of a nervous apprehension in her heart. She looked again at Julian. Was he doing something behind her back, something about which she knew nothing, yet was dimly aware of it? Like a shadow. *Was* there a shadow on the threshold of the Wreckers' House? She asked herself. *Was* he doing something behind her back, something which could harm her considerably?

He laughed.

'Good girl!' he said encouragingly. 'You know you and I have got to get on properly together. This is part of the job. In the next few weeks it would be as well if we kept nothing—and I mean nothing—from each other.'

'But of course. What is there to keep?'

'Exactly!'

They finished the meal almost in silence; somehow the conversation had run out and there was nothing more to say. She had found the old hypodermic needle in the ashtray, in her patient's writing-room. The patient herself could not have been well enough to use it, also she knew by Gay's condition that she had had something which she would have called 'different'. She herself had not given it. It could only have been the doctor or Julian. Julian had mentioned that at moments in extremity he had had to give Gay an injection. One of them had done it, but neither of them was going to tell her a thing.

It was hateful to think that something of this sort was going on in the Wreckers' House, something that she could not place or name.

114

What do I do? she thought.

All the time she knew that she was suspecting Julian Clare most of all, in spite of his amiable manner with her. He was a shade too slick, too highly polished, and far too sure of himself. He had admitted that earlier in his career he had wanted to be a doctor himself. He had told her with some pride that at least he had managed to last out the whole of his first year in hospital, and then had had to give in. It meant that he would have learnt a considerable amount of the preliminaries. Enough to give an injection, of course. He had laughed about the fact that he had left so soon; he had come to the conclusion that it was *not* really his career, and that he could never have stuck that eternity of time spent in training.

She told herself that she must not be too suspicious. It would not pay. She was here as a nurse, to obey the doctor and do the work as he prescribed it. It was quite wrong to have this latent feeling that behind it all was something that she did not understand. She must have been silent for quite a time, because suddenly Julian spoke to her.

'You're horribly quiet. Why?'

'I don't know.' But she did, of course. 'I suppose I was thinking what a glorious iced sweet they make here.'

'Yes old ma Janet *can* cook.'

'I find her a dear, and so fond of the patient.'

115

Julian pulled a face, and gave a little giggle. 'That's what *you* think. You wait till you know her a bit better! She's a proper old muddler, I'd say, not really my cup of tea.'

The savoury was brought in and handed round, then the butler paused in the doorway. 'Miss Sutcliffe desires me to tell you that I am to take the coffee up to her room after this, and she hopes that you will join her to have it there later on.'

'Yes, thank you.'

'Very good, sir,' and then he had gone, shutting the door behind him with that superb silence of the old retainer, who can always achieve this end, however hard the door may be to shut.

Julian had finished the savoury, and he pushed the plate aside. He lit a cigarette from the tall candle in the silver sconce standing at the corner of the table, an exquisitely moulded candle, and the flame was a tantalizing brilliant soft gamboge in colour. He said, a little patronizingly, 'You may not realize it as you have been here such a short time, but they say all of the wreckers' houses have strange personalities which live on in them, ghost personalities. I would not know. I worry for Gay. I am very fond of her, you see, always have been from the day when I first met her. I want her to get well.'

She smiled with real sympathy. 'Don't worry,

it never helps. It is something we all have to learn.'

'Not so easy to put it to one side.'

'I know,' and then very kindly she said, 'Suppose you tell me about it? Some of it, anyway? A worry shared is a worry already on the road to being cured. Why did you give up medicine?'

He evaded the truth. 'Because I am bone lazy, and first of all it was far too much like hard work, real hard work. Secondly, I hate death, and death was for ever in and out of the hospital. I could not bear it. I think curing in medicine is magnificent, and when I took it up it was with the idea of curing. I mean that.'

'I'm sure you do.'

'Then there were too many people for whom I could do nothing in the world, nothing at all, and that hurt me.' He lit another cigarette; when she came to think of it, there could be no end to the cigarettes he smoked in a single day, and it must be terribly bad for him. 'The urge did not last. Then they never let you be. One never seemed to be able to get a single moment to oneself, but was here, there and everywhere. To add to things, I have never had a first-class memory for names, and all those infernal drugs got me down. I had to learn their names by the string. I can tell you, it isn't funny.'

She nodded. 'I failed in that myself the first time, and we nurses get a mere third of the

117

quantity that you men have to learn. I do understand how that worried you.'

He was at this moment quite a nice man, someone who she had never suspected lay beneath the rest of him. 'I hate people dying,' he said, 'I suppose I always shall, and this is idiotic, because people have to die to make room for the new people coming into the world. I sound a casual person, one of the kind that do not bother too much, but I do bother about things, and I . . . well, I was never fitted to be a doctor, if you ask me, so I gave it up.'

'You are happy without it?'

He laughed then, like a boy. 'I am a damned sight happier than I ever was *with* it,' he said. Then he changed the subject. 'I wonder you stuck it out, a pretty girl like you.'

'I very nearly didn't,' she admitted. 'I also had my bad moments, maybe we all do, when I longed to go home; if I had had a home, but that was something I hadn't really got.'

'That is why you are so impressed with the Wreckers' House?'

'Maybe.'

He got up then. 'Gay'll be waiting. She has had one of her trying days and needs a little fun now. Let's go to her.'

As they went out of the beautiful dining-room with the candles lit, and their pale yellow flames showing more clearly as the dusk crept up and over the garden, she thought what a charming

118

place this was. The house had real beauty; one could not associate it with wreckers, and the havoc they had caused. She led the way out of the dining-room and up the wide stairway which rose from the far end of the hall. The stairs were of oak. It was strange that the quiet almost comforting beauty of this place could ever have belonged to ruthless people like the wreckers, murderers who did not hesitate to run a knife into an enemy, or a friend if it came to that! It was such a lovely house now, admirably managed, and with fresh flowers in every room with the new morning, and a superb sense of happiness reigned over it. One could never imagine that a wicked thought had ever come here, but it had done, as she well knew. They went along the wide corridor with the pictures on the walls, Gay's own paintings, and to the room at the far end.

Gay was sitting up in bed now, propped by the specially big pillows that she had. The curious thing was that she always recovered so quickly after a really diabolical attack, and now you would never have dreamt what a shockingly bad day she had had. Her hair had been brushed back and piled high, and she smiled as they entered the room.

'Lovely to see you,' she said.

They sat down on either side of her, and beside her the window was wide open. Beyond it lay the sea, miles of it with that soft greyness on the horizon, that faint lingering impression of something there that one could not quite see. The water was that faint blue which comes to that sea, and the strong sweet smell of the garden flowers (always stronger at this hour of the night) came in through the windows. Looking at the garden below, the calmly translucent sea, and the general air of peace which somehow entered the room and added to their sweetness, it was hard to believe that men had been kept prisoner here.

Alan Thane had been along to see Gay whilst they were eating. It seemed that he was a visitor to this house who entered by the side door, and if he found no one about, left again. He was accepted almost as an elder son, and came and went, bringing books with him. Bridget had never seen a woman who read so much as Gay Sutcliffe, for she read by the hour.

'We never heard him,' said Julian rather sharply, almost as if he was displeased.

'No, of course not, but then he has a free pass to the house, you know, and comes and goes as he wishes. I should die without his books. He has more than anyone else I know, and can always advise me about the right one to read.'

'I was never that fond of reading,' said Julian a trifle sulkily. He had had to read too much at hospital, read and learn by heart. As he said, 'And if ever you want to be put off a book well and truly, that is the way to do it.'

'Alan did not stay. He has had trouble on the farm. He lost two of his best sheep this week, and does not know quite why. He gets very disturbed for his animals,' she said quietly. 'Besides, financially, it is quite a big loss.'

'Yes, of course.'

She was in a happy mood now. She had tremendous powers of recovery directly the pain had gone, for she was one of those people who can contrive to draw down a curtain, and think no more about it. She said she could shut it right out of her life. She talked of the local fête which would be held next month, and the wild effort to get somebody to open it who would draw in the crowds. They held their fêtes at this time of the year when you could hardly get another visitor on to the Cornish coast.

'But sometimes I think that when winter comes, those sharp days, and when there is snow, then this sea looks at its best. That is when the most wonderful lights come to it.' Then she paused. She spoke again in a lower voice. 'Last night I had been lying here reading, the sun had not yet set but was falling, when I looked up, and I saw a mirage!'

'You're always seeing something!' Julian said.

'No, this really was. Palm trees, a few huts, the sort of straw-thatched huts I should imagine those people have. It was along the horizon. I simply could not believe my eyes, and lay there staring at it. I had never seen a mirage before.

The locals had told me that you could see them here, sometimes, not often of course, yet when I looked at it I could not believe my eyes.'

'It's supposed to bring people luck,' Julian said.

'I need some of that!'

Bridget went closer. 'I hope maybe that I have brought you some,' she said, 'for that is what I want to do.'

'You *have* brought me luck. I felt you would the moment I first saw you,' and the patient smiled.

That was when there was a knock at the door. It was not the butler, he of course would have been occupied with tidying up after the dinner, but the little maid. She had come to say that Alan Thane had returned. He had had some books brought down from London by car, and amongst them was one he knew that Gay very much wanted to read.

Gay looked up. She had had a good deal of pain today and felt limp with it. Bridget got up.

'I'll slip down and see him. I can explain,' she said.

'That would be good of you.'

'Don't worry that he won't understand. He is one of the most understanding people I have ever met,' and she said it gaily.

Bridget went along the corridor and down the wide stairway. Alan was waiting in the hall on the far side of it, and seeing him there she again felt the sudden pang—and for no reason—the pang that she had felt when she had seen the hypodermic needle (a used one, for it was slightly twisted) lying in the ashtray in her patient's writing-room. It was extremely odd that the memory should come back to her at this moment, the moment when she had just been talking to her patient, but it did.

Alan wore fawn slacks and thick boots. He had on one of those very soft blue sweaters of which he seemed to be particularly fond. He walked towards her, the book in his hand.

'I've come at an awkward moment?' he said. He had a faculty for conveying his own feelings, which made one trust him. The deep-set eyes were vividly blue as he spoke. 'I am so sorry if I disturbed things, when I came earlier. She had had a bad day and was only just recovered. She is good at recovery. She wanted this book, and I was not expecting it, but a special friend got it for me and I wished her to have it.'

'I'll take it to her. She rather hoped you had it. She has had a difficult afternoon with bad pain, and I was out when it came on. Mr. Clare took me to see some of the sights. Cornwall is very wonderful.'

'All that, and a bit more. Is she better now?'

'Oh yes, it is moving off, and she should not have another attack for quite a while. She is watching the sea, she loves doing that.'

'I know she does. She adores the house, too.

123

When she first bought it, it was said to be haunted. But she did not care, and has made it absolutely charming.'

'She has indeed.'

'If you had seen it then . . . !'

'I know. Tell me, were the wreckers very bad people, as men say? They are new to me, because in the inland counties I suppose they seem to be remote, something more like a fairy tale than real.'

'They were no fairy tales. Here men died. They did unbelievably cruel work, murdered men in their hundreds, got out and changed the lights so that the charts betrayed the sailors, and ships went on to the rocks before they realized what had happened to them. Nobody can speak badly enough of the wreckers. Then they sneaked the cargo.'

'Valuable?'

'Oh yes, contraband of all sorts, rich cargoes out of which they could make a fortune for themselves, and they did. The wreckers did not care if their brothers and sisters and their fathers went down to the bottom of the sea never to be seen again. It did not worry a wrecker what he did, as long as he got his reward.'

She nodded. 'Pretty awful!'

'Awful without being particularly pretty!' he agreed, and then he asked her a surprise question, which somehow she had never expected to come from him. 'You like Julian

124

Clare?'

She was so startled that she felt herself colouring, for she did not like him. 'Well, not very much. . . . Why?'

'He appeared on the scene here, living in the house, about four years back. Gay is one of those people who adore youth, and she would do anything to help young people. He painted quite nicely. I believe it all began when he met her out at Innsbrück, and then they became great friends. You would have thought that their tastes were as the poles apart.'

Bridget said, 'I know, but they get along well together.'

'Yes, and he can manage her.'

She agreed, and inwardly was glad that somebody else had noticed this. He stood there, hands dug into his pockets, looking at her, yet in some strange way *not* looking at her.

He said, 'I gather that recently she made a will in his favour, leaving him everything, and all future royalties on her books. I don't like the sound of that too much.'

'Yes, I believe that is the case.'

Half of her told herself that Sister Tutor would never forgive such a confession to what she would have called 'an outsider', yet somehow Bridget had felt that he needed the truth. She had known from the first moment she had walked into this house that there was something peculiar about it. The house itself was lovely, but behind it all there was still the feeling of the vilest men in the world who had robbed and had slain. It was odd, but the one man whom she could trust, stood before her. A man wearing a soft blue sweater, with a polo neck to it, and kind eyes which searched her.

She said suddenly, 'I don't understand what is happening here, for I have been in the house far too short a time, but there *is* something funny afoot. I . . . I am not at all sure of the treatment.'

'But I thought you knew the medicines?'

She shook her head.

For a single moment she realized how much she needed help. She could trust this man, she had known it from the very beginning, and she began to talk. He was born honest as the way is long, she knew this, and she began to discuss what had happened. 'I am not happy; something is going on which I do not understand, and I want to understand it, yet do not know whom to ask or what to do.'

She spoke then of Dr. Forbes, a curious man, a man who had the faculty of living behind a mask. You never got a single clue as to what he was thinking, and in medicine it is urgent that doctor and nurse should understand each other. There was a wall between herself and this man, something she could not hope to tear down. She paused, then she went on again, and all the time Alan was watching her as she spoke, but his blue eyes were kind, he understood her worry, and she knew that he would do anything he could for her.

She spoke quickly; one does when really worried. She spoke of how she had glanced down at the little ashtray—Gay smoked only on rare occasions for she did not like cigarettes, she just had one when the pain had been too bad—and lying in the tray there was just a little ash, sufficient for one cigarette. Then she had seen the sudden gleam, the flash of steel, she supposed, a used hypodermic needle.

'My patient is having something about which I know nothing, and although I have seen the doctor since, and tried to help him to tell me, I had no success. One has to be careful, he is a difficult man whom I do not understand, and who in some ways is alarming. He knew nothing about it apparently, just turned haughty. I know he doesn't like me.'

'I should not jump to conclusions. He is a man with a rather awkward manner and always shows the worst of himself. He did not know?'

'I am almost sure he had not got a clue. He just pushed it aside, and said she had had no injection; by the way he said it, I should have thought he considered that to be the truth. It sounded like it to me.' She was half ashamed of admitting this, yet somehow this evening she had come to the conclusion that she had to tell somebody. Circumstances were closing in around her, and she was afraid.

'Is that all?' he asked her.

'Yes, all that really matters, but I have the feeling that things are not quite what they seem. There is nothing concrete, nothing that I could possibly produce, but I have this feeling all the time. I find Julian Clare a difficult man. He was a medical student for a time.'

'I didn't know that. He has never told me.'

'He worked for a year at hospital, so I believe. I am not sure, but that is what he said.'

'It does complicate things.'

'Her death would help him?'

He nodded. 'She changed her will, and tells the world that he inherits the lot. I believe this to be true.'

'And he is not rich?'

'I don't know.'

She thought of the way Janet disliked him, and if she had been given the chance to talk would have told all sorts of stories. Janet said that Julian never paid a bill in his life because he did not like doing it; he thought it was the best way to waste money! The result was, of course, that he had an extremely bad name in the neighbourhood. 'Janet does not trust him, and the awful thing is that ever since I saw that needle in the ashtray, I do not trust him either. I almost asked the doctor without actually saying that I knew, but he betrayed nothing.'

They talked on for a while, then he returned

to the subject and said that for the moment she must hold her peace.

'But something ought to be done.'

'Nothing now. Something must be done, but for the time being we could only commit ourselves. Think of me as a friend, someone in the background who loves the patient and wants to help.' They started to walk towards the door together. The day had nearly died and the sea had turned grey with the lighthouses lit up, their beams of light shimmering everywhere, going, but even returning.

'One moment, do go up and see her,' she said, and that was when the telephone shrilled and she had to go to it. She heard a man's voice at the far end of the line. 'It is Nurse speaking,' she said.

'It is Nurse with whom I would have a word. This is Frank Dene. How are you, Bridget? I'm the chap who got you the job, so don't say you have already forgotten me!'

'Never! Of course not! Where are you?'

'That is exactly why I have rung up. I have a patient at St. Ives of all places, and shall be coming your way tomorrow. I've booked in at the inn. How is Gay?'

'This has been a bad day, but she's better now,' and then with the spontaneity of which Bridget had not believed herself to be capable, 'You are just the person I most want to see. Thank God you are coming down, for you can help me.'

'Nothing has gone wrong?'

'Nothing externally, nothing one could lay a finger on, but I have a feeling that something *is* wrong here. I am so glad you are coming.'

'Tell her possibly tomorrow morning.'

'I will. Alan Thane is with her now.'

'He's a good chap. I'll see them in the morning and shall stay a couple of nights at the Dolphin and hear the news. Good-bye.'

As she hung up the receiver Bridget felt better and almost as if a miracle had happened, and the fairies were helping her. As she turned away she saw Alan coming down the stairs.

'Good news,' she said, 'Frank Dene is seeing a patient in St. Ives and coming on here tomorrow.'

'That's a help.' She saw the strongly cut face of the man change as he laughed, and the eyes brightened. 'He is the man to help us out of this hole, because I have a hunch that we *are* in a hole.'

'So have I,' she said.

This was good news, for he was the man with whom one could talk, the man in whom one could confide. She went back to her patient, now much recovered, and a far better colour than she had been before. She told her what had happened, and instantly Gay cheered up.

'He is seeing someone in St. Ives, leaving first thing in the morning and coming straight here,'

Bridget said.

'He must stay here with me. Oh, I do wish he would.'

'He says he has booked in at the inn. He likes it there.'

Gay smiled. 'I can't think why he won't stay here, but I am overjoyed that he is coming.'

She reflected her own joy, and beamed with pleasure. She told of their friendship, for they had known each other since they were in their 'teens. She was sure that he had done more for her than anybody else in the world, and was always so kind. She insisted that Janet must get all his pet food, she had a genius for remembering people's favourite puddings.

Last thing of all Julian joined them. He came into the room looking sour. 'Now what has gone wrong with him?' Bridget asked herself, for there seemed to be no reason for it. Instantly Gay, overflowing with the good news which was exciting her, told him what she had heard, and of her glee that tomorrow would bring a dear old friend back into the house. Julian said exactly nothing, then when Gay queried this, remarked, 'I'd have thought he would have bored you stiff, but there you are!'

'I'll fetch the hot water bottle,' Bridget said. It was merely an excuse, of course, just one of those things which happen in this hard world. When she took the hot water bottle upstairs, she said it would be wise for Gay to have an early night after a sickeningly painful day. Julian had left her, he was a man who read a lot in bed, so possibly he had gone to his room. There was no sign of their having quarrelled or anything of that kind. As she said good night, Bridget said that as it was so lovely out she was taking the dog for a last walk round.

'You're good to him.'

'I have always loved dogs, and it is such a grand night. A walk round the fields, and then I'll be back. I won't disturb you again,' she promised.

She went downstairs, the dog with her. She walked across the road into the fields belonging to Alan, and walked near the hedges. The ditches were thick with wild flowers, which smelt sweetly, and she stayed to pick some honeysuckle, which at this time of the evening was superb. That was when she saw Alan approaching her. He also had been walking round the fields, which she knew he did frequently. At this hour when the hush had come, when the cows were lying there resting, and the sheep under the trees asleep, there was a tranquillity which had a rare beauty of its own.

'Gay and Frank are very old friends?' asked Bridget after a moment.

'Almost all their lives.'

'And you have lived here all your life?'

He had, indeed. His people had come here at the time of fat, little Queen Anne. He said he would never choose to live anywhere else. The farmhouse where now he lived was a beautifully built house with lovely gardens, and had originally been a couple of cottages built at that very time, and subsequently added to.

They talked quietly, then she went home.

She had a key to the door, for the old butler would have gone to bed. She went in through the side door, and there was that superb peace about the place which comes at this time of night. She went up the smaller stairway, for this had a thick carpet on it, and she did not want to upset anybody. As she got to the landing (the little back landing with the door opening on to the main floor), she heard a man speaking. It was Julian's voice. He was speaking in a low tone, and the man he spoke to was the doctor. 'What is he doing here now?' she asked herself, for it was five minutes to midnight, an absurd hour at which to pay a visit.

'A good thing we understand each other,' he was saying.

'It's the girl who worries me. There was no need for her to come, and the sooner she goes back the better.'

'She's going back, whatever my aunt says,' and he gave a laugh, and then said something in a whisper.

She felt her hand turn clammy on the door.

CHAPTER SIX

The curious thing was that Bridget slept late. She had thought that she would never sleep at all, she thought it had served her right to have heard something unpleasant, for when she was a child her mother had insisted to her that 'listeners never hear any good for themselves'.

She dressed quickly and went to the patient. Janet had brought up her breakfast. It was one of those perfect days, with the hot sunshine pouring into the window, the sea pale blue and flat, never so much as a single sign of a wave on it. Gay was feeling so much better that she said she would dress and get into her wheel-chair.

'I want to go into the garden,' she said. 'It always looks quite lovely on a day like this; come along with me.'

So they went together, with Gay in the chair. She was excited that Frank Dene was coming, for she had the greatest faith in him and longed to see him. The garden was already quite hot in the sunshine, and smelt of the loveliest flowers of all the year.

She talked of the wreck it had been when she bought it. A barn, whose roof had crashed in, and lay in a pile of old slates and tiles on the ground. How she had gone into every detail. The architects were not too pleased about her ideas, and had told her that she would never achieve her end. But she did! All the neighbourhood insisted that the place was haunted, and one of these days she would be worried to death that she had ever come here.

'But I am not like that,' she said. 'I am not a person who is susceptible to ghosts. I have never been scared of them, if there are such things. Sometimes I think they are just shadows cast by the past, nothing real at all. I came here because I loved the house.'

'And to me, in spite of everything that I hear about it, it is a *kind* house,' said the girl.

'You are right there, that is exactly what it is, a kind house. Years ago when the Lord of the Manor lived here, it was a very grand house indeed; then it fell into disrepair, and the wreckers got it. They were never good to houses, and just hacked them about. I daresay men died here, they would not have cared, but that bad time is over.'

'And you have never been afraid of it?'

'No,' and she laughed. She had perhaps the most attractive house in all the world. 'I opened up all the windows, so that the fresh air and the sunshine came into it. I felt the place needed this. They are even open on to the sea itself, and today it is happy. There are extra rooms for stores, and one of these days I shall turn them into spare bedrooms, so that I can have friends galore to stay here. I love friends, you see.'

It would be a bright idea to have more spare bedrooms. Bridget turned back to work, and looked after her patient. Later in the day she returned a book to Alan's farm. She took Smutty, and they went together. The farm had attraction, and now with the jasmine in full flower, casting out its eternal lovely scent, it seemed like heaven itself. Alan was walking in the garden, and came to meet them.

'You should not have bothered to bring the book back.'

'Gay wished it, so I came. She says that it is an enchanting book, she loved it.'

'Yes, it is about this part of the world, so of course it held her fast. She is a very keen reader, like me. The joy is that we both like the same sort of books, and find them good fun. *You* ought to write.'

She thought of that as she went home to Gay and laughingly told her what Alan had said. 'And why don't you try?' Gay asked.

'I suppose there is always a ready reader for a good book,' she said, 'but I doubt if I could write a really good book. I'd love to write of the wreckers.'

'If that is the way you feel, yes, of course, for they were a strange people. Do you know much about them?'

'Nothing, but I'm fascinated.'

'Alan would lend you a big store of books, for he has heaps of them.'

It was curious that quite suddenly the idea had struck her, and hard. She said, 'I'll have a talk with him,' and knew that she blushed gaily. 'Oh, I *should* enjoy it! I really should.'

'In an emergency, I am here to help.' Gay Sutcliffe laughed at the idea.

Bridget busied herself about her work, tidying the room for the night, for she knew by the look of things that Gay was getting tired, and would probably want to go to bed early. One had to be careful for her. When she had done, however, Gay had gone to her desk. She had had another idea for the book on which she was engaged, and had wandered back there to it. Bridget went back to the garden to get some more flowers to stand beside the patient's bed. She renewed these every night. She gathered some of the jasmine which smelt so lovely, some soft pink roses, that tender first pink which is so beautiful, and some little white anemones which grew in a side bed.

She saw Julian returning from fishing, for he had been out again with the doctor.

'No luck,' he said, 'I don't know what is the matter with the sea just now, but there is not a fish to be had.'

'Better luck tomorrow?' she suggested.

'And what have you been doing?'

'Messing about. Talking about books with Miss Sutcliffe. She rather wants *me* to write one about the wreckers.'

He laughed at that. 'Do you know much about them?'

'Less than I should have thought possible, but she says that it would be all right. One never knows, of course.'

'And who will publish it?'

'I wasn't even worrying about that one.'

'You may find that you will *have* to worry about that one, for a book without a publisher is clean lost. It is wasted, unless somebody produces it.'

'She thinks that perhaps. . . .'

He linked an arm in hers, somehow she disliked it, perhaps because the coat that he was wearing smelt of fish, and she did not care for it very much. He said, 'A book without a publisher is a new-born baby without life, and that is the truth. Gay knows that just as everybody else dos.'

'But some books get published.'

'Some. Not all. Very many less than all,' he said.

She moved her arm away, murmured something about having a job to do, and went up to the room with the flowers. She wished that she was not one of those people who are so easily disappointed, of whom there are far too many in the world. She wished that she did not take things to heart. She found Gay happily writing; one had to admit that when the spirit moved her, it made her amazingly happy and quite a different woman. Then when she got her to bed, she was worn out, and could hardly eat her supper because she was so exhausted.

'You *need* food,' Bridget said.

'I never feel like eating after I have just written myself out.'

'Perhaps you should not do so much. Perhaps that is the trouble. Next time, leave off before the tiredness comes.' Then when she had helped her through the meal, she left her with the radio playing. They were doing an interesting Beethoven programme, one which Miss Sutcliffe was very fond of, and this would possibly lull her off.

'You've got the loveliest ideas,' she said.

'I try to think for my patients.'

'You're a pet.'

She noticed half an hour later that her patient was asleep, which was what she wanted, and she went to sit in the garden with Julian Clare. He could be so pleasant at times, so very different from the other side of his nature. He talked of Gay with real interest. He doted on her and always had done. He talked of the doctor; somehow Bridget always thought of him as 'the young doctor', and she did not know why, because he must be in the early fifties.

'He is brilliant with her.'

'I wish she had some more advanced treatment. I am sure more could be done. There are new ideas in hospitals now.'

Julian glanced at her. 'Gay is nervous of new things. She has suffered so much already, poor thing. It's understandable that she is afraid of what she undertakes if it has not been fully proved.'

She nodded. She went on, 'I am so glad that Mr. Dene is coming to see us, he has been so good to me.' Somehow she did not like the way he looked at her, almost as if his eyes were trying to read right through her, right *into* her. As though there was something that he did not understand, and perhaps did not want to understand.

Cautiously, and without saying a single word, Julian poured himself out another drink. 'Well, well, well!' was what he ultimately said. 'And he might suggest something new, you think?'

'Well, yes, I do.'

He said nothing, just sat there twirling the glass round in his fingers, almost as if he did not believe it. Then he said, 'I hope not. Hubert Forbes would hate someone else butting in.'

'But he *is* a specialist.'

'E.N.T., if I remember rightly.'

'You are perfectly right. At the same time this particular complaint has always been a great interest of his. She ought to have every chance there is, more, if we could find it,' and then in a sudden burst, something that she felt deep down in her very heart, 'She is too nice to die. Far far too nice to be afflicted like this.'

'Yes, of course; all the same I wish he was not coming down. I must tell Hubert.'

'He cannot mind?'

'I don't see why not.' He went quiet and for a moment she thought he was angry with her, and hated it.

They went indoors, and the old man brought the coffee in and put it before them. He said that he understood that Miss Sutcliffe was still asleep, and therefore it would be wise not to disturb her. In a way, somehow she felt that they had reached a danger point. She was still thinking about that hypodermic needle that she had seen in the ashtray. The doctor knew nothing of it, that was quite plain; she could only think that Gay Sutcliffe had used it herself, which was extremely unlikely, or that Julian knew a good deal more of it than he would ever say. She was going on worrying until she found the answer.

She wondered if Julian could read thoughts. It almost seemed like it. He was drinking his coffee very slowly, a man who sipped it, when he said, 'If you want to take some good advice, Bridget, you will perhaps realize once and for all that it is not quite wise to try to interfere with the treatment of private patients. I wouldn't butt in. Let well alone. Gay is being admirably looked after, I can promise you that.'

'I am sure she is.'

It was, of course, crazy to suspect him, yet

deep down in her heart this was what she was doing. There was some quality about him which she did not like, something which she did not understand. He was the heir to everything, a lucky young man, for the royalties on Gay's books would continue for many years after her death, without a doubt. Bridget was here filling an appointment, and what he said was true. She must not suspect and yet at the same time she was suspecting somebody.

They finished the coffee, talking of other things. Alan and the farm which had belonged to him and his people for many generations and was said to be one of the most profitable on this side of the county. Julian had known of him ever since he had first come to stay in the neighbourhood, which had been seven or eight years ago.

They must have sat there talking much longer than they had thought, for the door opened and Janet appeared. She was in something of a tizzy. Apparently Miss Sutcliffe had had her coffee upstairs alone, and had fallen sound asleep over it. Janet had slipped upstairs and had sneaked it away, and Miss Sutcliffe had later asked when she was going to have it, and refused to believe that she had already had it. She wanted her nurse and adopted nephew to come up, and she wanted more coffee brought to her now.

She would not be denied.

Not sure of what to do, Janet had come in to

the other two, who said the best possible thing was for them to take up some coffee with them, pretend they had never had theirs, and get on with it.

'Very well, sir,' said Janet to Julian.

'I'll explain it all if it has to be explained, but I expect it will be quite all right.'

They went upstairs together.

They entered the bedroom with the radio still playing Beethoven, as Bridget had left it. Gay looked far better for the rest, and was delighted to see them.

'I went sound asleep and lost my coffee, but I wasn't having that one!' she said gaily, 'and Janet is bringing some up for all of us. Nice to see you. It has been something of a worrying day.'

'I thought it had been a lovely day,' Bridget said.

They sat down one on either side of her, and after a little while she started to talk about a new book she was thinking of writing. She always liked discussing new books first, and getting several people's opinions on them, before she actually began. Later, when she got started, she never asked anything more, but wrote as fast as her crippled hand would allow. Once she got going, there was no end to it for her, and she would continue until she almost collapsed. Bridget marvelled at the tremendous thrill which seemed to inspire her.

She talked now. She saw the book almost like some remarkable picture before her, was intrigued by it, in love with it, and prepared to give unending time to it.

She said, 'You think it would be all right?'

'But of course.' It was Julian who spoke. 'You always get the most ravishing ideas. How do they come?'

In a low voice she said, 'This house is very kind to me. It has many tales to tell. I ... I think this new idea will be all right, I hope so. It is so difficult at first.'

Bridget asked her, 'Do you actually see the book when you are thinking about it, like people see pictures in the cinema? Something that unfolds itself before you? It's hard to explain.'

'She writes down notes whilst she remembers it,' Julian said. 'Sometimes she sleeps on it and forgets it next day, and that is shocking.'

'I write it all down,' said Gay. 'Once I learnt shorthand but I'm horribly bad at it and prefer my own wobbly hand.'

She started off writing, and Bridget had never thought that she could go on so long, for she went on and on, gaining speed as the story possessed her, took hold of her and made itself clear. Finally, when she had finished, Bridget said, 'You must be tired out.'

Julian had already slipped away, and they were alone.

'Oh no, not really. One never gets tired of

one's own stories, they come, and they thrill one. But *you* must be tired. You did all that work.'

'I love my job.'

Gay looked at her, keenly interested and ready to help, then she said, 'Bring me that little box off the dressing-table, and my little handbag. I have got the key in that.' She brought both of them and set them on the bed beside her. Gay opened the box, it was a white leather one lined with a pale blue silk, and inside it there were trays of brooches and jewels, pieces that she loved. She picked out a brooch; it was a single blue flower made of aquamarines, and with tiny emeralds on the stalk as leaves. 'To bring you luck,' was what she said, very intently, as one wanting to help. 'I think it might bring you the luck I want for you, for you are a dear girl.'

Bridget did not know what to say.

Then spontaneously she put both arms round her patient and kissed her. 'You—you're a darling,' she said.

She thought a lot about her that night, for somehow she did not sleep too easily. She was worried. Still at the back of her mind there lurked that hypodermic needle which she had not been able to explain yet dare not speak about. She had had from the first the strange feeling that there was something that was *wrong* in this house, something which stayed here and

145

could not be brought into the open. They were all nice people on the face of things. She liked Alan Thane enormously, and she counted on him as being someone who was quite separate from the rest of them. It was undoubtedly not Alan. She did not care for Julian Clare, for somehow she had the feeling that he was changeable, that he did not always speak the truth, and that he was odd with her.

Outwardly he seemed to be very fond of Gay, but she had done so much for him that surely he could not possibly feel different? He had had some medical training, that was the thought that kept vibrating through her, penetrating right down into her very heart, and possessing her. He would know how to use a hypodermic, how to give an injection, and quite possibly quite a lot about the drug to give. A student in those first few months had to learn a great deal. He had admitted this.

He had probably left because he had got sick of being worked so hard, and she knew that these men did work hard. He had blamed his memory; one had to have a good memory, without a doubt, one had to know what one was talking about, and also the Warden was fairly sharp with the medical students. She sometimes wondered how any of them tolerated it, save that men were more used to authority than women.

When Julian had forgone being a doctor, and

at the end of the first year as a student had thought it futile, what job had he taken up? Nothing at all, she understood.

He had been abroad for a time, so Janet had told her. He went to live with a friend in Australia for a while, a woman much older than he was, for he was a man who preferred older folk. She died while he was with her.

'How awful for him!' Bridget said to Janet.

'Yes, Nurse, I suppose so.' But there was something odd about the way she said it. Later Gay Sutcliffe mentioned it. The woman who had died had been a distant relative, for she had married a cousin who went out there to live. He had fallen out of love with modern England.

She talked of the woman, who had been very charming, an artist at one time doing very well, and people had discussed her work. Then she had married this old cousin and they had gone to Australia where she had given up painting. Gay thought it a pity to waste talent. The woman had been broken-hearted when the old man died, and that was when Julian had gone to visit her. She was having heart attacks and needed help. He had gone originally on a brief visit, but he must have been with her for a whole couple of years when she died in one of her heart attacks. She had left him all she had, and he had sold up and returned to England.

When Gay told the story, Bridget disliked it. Somehow it gave her a sense of insecurity and of doubt. She was suspicious, and had always hated the fact that Julian gave Gay her medicines.

Privately Bridget knew that Janet also was worried for her mistress.

This was a strange world. She slept late next day, another of those brilliant hot days of which they seemed to have so many here, a day of light turquoise, and a mist out at sea, and far away the complaining sound of a ship resenting the fog.

But today she would be seeing Frank Dene again, she told herself, and he was one of those men who was absolutely trustworthy. But he could be erratic, and experience at hospital had taught her that he could often appear long before expected, but whatever he did it would be enchanting to see him again. There were things they must speak of. Those injections, what ought she to do? To say? What could she do for a patient who was in the hands of another person in the house, someone whom she did not trust?

One thing was certain.

She was going to talk the whole affair out with Frank Dene whatever happened. He must know what was going on and advise her. She would also like to discuss the new drug with him, for the tests in hospital had been favourable, and so far she herself was all for it. She knew that Gay would try anything, in spite of what Julian had said to the contrary, but she must be sure that the patient was well advised.

She had finished her breakfast and had gone upstairs to prepare Gay for the day, and for the visitor whom she was so looking forward to seeing. That was when the little maid came and asked her to come downstairs for Mr. Thane was here and asking for her.

'For me, or for Miss Sutcliffe?'

The little girl was not quite sure but thought it might be for both of them. Miss Sutcliffe said she did not feel quite up to visitors for the moment, would Bridget go down and find out what it was, and let her know later?

She went down the side staircase with the lovely slender stairs, which you find only in very old stairways. The hall was lit by the morning sun. Here and there were big divan sofas with crimson velvet on them, and heavy matching cushions everywhere. In the big old-fashioned fireplace there stood a tremendous bowl of blue delphiniums, tall and splendid in spires. Pale and dark blue, and some with that faint mauve beauty attached to them. They looked magnificent.

There was something spoiling about the sheer beauty of the place and everything that it offered. One could never imagine that the ridiculous word 'wreckers' ever had anything to do with this sweet house, for it was so lovely. One could not imagine this house those hundred and more years back when men had died here, when men had been dragged in dying, and where those appalling wreckers had worked for profit with the ships passing to and fro.

But now it had the quality of real beauty with the sunshine pouring in, the heavy refectory table which was of enormous length, and with more tall vases of these dazzling blue delphiniums.

Alan was standing by the centre table, looking at a magazine which had been lying there. He wore fawn slacks, and thick shoes, and a pale blue jumper, which suited him so well. He was quite fiercely bronzed, a man for ever out in the sunshine, and never wearing a hat. He was tanned by the sun, and his eyes had that vivid gleam in them which had been one of the very first things she had noticed about him.

He looked up at once.

'I am so sorry if I have upset things by coming across too early, I gather Miss Sutcliffe was not too well. She very much wanted to get a peep at this book, so she said, and as it came down to me this morning from London I thought I would lose no time in bringing it over. I hope I have not done the wrong thing.'

'Of course not. She had a bit of a worry yesterday, I think that upset her.' She indicated the dark red divan sofa by her side. 'Sit down for a moment, do? She had a rough day yesterday, but she has her doctor friend coming down here today and she is saving up her strength for this. *I* had a wonderful day yesterday, for I went out in the car with Julian Clare. It really is the most enchanting county.'

'Yes, it is. It is a county which never minds its age being known, and this is what I like about it. But then I am a Cornishman, so of course I find it all wonderful.'

'It is unbelievable.'

'And Miss Sutcliffe is better today?'

'Oh yes, much better, and I hope that Mr. Dene can help her. He's a dear.'

'She needs help, real help,' and he said it quite gravely.

'You have known her for some time?'

'Yes, I have—longer than I care to think. She bought this place over twelve years ago. It was chaotic then, falling down, practically in pieces. It hardly seemed worth repairing, because it was in ruins. She was intrigued about it and came here to ask me for advice. It was exciting working on the house with her. Now I hope she is living happily in it. If only we could rid her of this wretched illness, then she would have everything. Everything there is.'

Bridget did not know how she dared ask, but she did. 'How did you get to know Julian Clare? I mean, was he here when she first came, or did he join her after? It—it all seems a little odd to me, I don't know why, and of course it is no business of mine really, but there is something

about him which worries me, and ... and ...'
she ended a trifle lamely. 'I am a bit concerned.'

He smiled.

'I can understand how you feel. Miss Sutcliffe
was here on and off for about five years. It took
four before the house was fit to live in, and then
only part of it. It had been in the most terrible
state of disrepair. Then he came to visit her. She
is one of those people who adore youth, and she
loves young people. I feel that Julian is
infectiously young, though not all that young in
years. At first I thought he was not her sort, but
apparently I was wrong.'

Still guardedly, for she was anxious, Bridget
said, 'I think somehow that he knows how to
manage her. That rather worries me. He is a
charming personality, of course, and is most
kind to her, there is really nothing that he
wouldn't do for her, but at the same time it is
worrying, leastways to me.'

There was a second's silence, then Alan
Thane said, 'In some ways to me also. I was
never too sure of the friendship. I may be
making a shocking mistake, for as you say, he
has been good to her, and I might be mistaken in
feeling as I do. I believe that now she looks upon
him as her real nephew.'

'Yes she says so.'

'And has left him everything. Mind you, this
happened before with a lady friend he had on
the other side of the world, and went out there

to be with her, and ... well ... she left him the lot!'

'He's a very lucky young man,' said Bridget slowly, but she was unhappy about things. She did not know quite what to say or do next. She could feel between the two of them a barrier of reserve, something that she did not understand.

Alan was looking at her. There was something very kind about his face, something sympathetic about the eyes which watched her, and at that moment she knew that there was nothing in the world with which she would not trust him. He said very quietly, 'Look here, I can see you are worried; supposing you tell me what it is? I can keep a secret, you know,' he smiled.

For a single moment she held back, and then she spoke again of the hypodermic needle which she had found in the ashtray beside her patient's desk. Already the girl knew sufficient of Miss Sutcliffe to know that she would never cheat. If she had used it herself, she would have admitted it, without a doubt. There was something peculiar going on in this house. Something to which for the moment she had no clue, and she was dismayed. When she had finished she just said no more. After a long pause Alan spoke,

'Is that all? Still worrying about the syringe?' he asked.

'There is one more thing, but for the present I am keeping quiet about that. I feel as if in some extraordinary way there is something else that is very wrong in this house. It is a kind house, but the spirit of the wreckers is still here. I am sure they have never quite gone. I don't mean ghosts, I don't mean anything particular, or supernatural, or unreal, but just that in a way the spirit of the wreckers is here, in this house, without a doubt. I am sure of it.'

He nodded. 'Only that isn't possible. One must stick to the bounds of possibility, you know. This is a kind house, as you say. I am sure that not for a single moment would it hurt you or yours. If you want the truth, I have mistrusted Julian Clare from the very first time I met him, and I admit that I have no reason for it, none at all.'

'I ... I am glad that you feel this way, for it helps me,' and for the first time she smiled.

He went on talking.

'I know all this is difficult. We are playing with fire, and fire burns, given the chance. But I have always found in life that when one is in a real corner, sooner or later Fate puts out a hand and helps one out. Life has always worked that way for me, and could work for you too the first time it gets the chance. It is a comforting thought.'

'I wonder. I feel a bit frightened.'

It was at that moment that the telephone shrilled on the table at her side, and the girl turned to it and picked up the receiver.

'The Wreckers' House,' she said.

'Who is speaking?'

'Miss Sutcliffe's nurse, Bridget Smythe.'

'That you, Bridget? Guess who it is here!' and even as he said this she recognized the voice, and the whole of her heart seemed to leap up inside her. 'This is Frank Dene.'

'We are expecting you today.'

'It can't be today after all. I am so sorry but I have an op. to do. It's only a small one, and I shall be along tomorrow for sure.'

'She'll be disappointed over the delay, but enchanted that you are coming anyway.'

'I shall spend two nights at the local.'

'Gay won't like that, I'm sure that she would want you here; there are lovely bedrooms and bathrooms, it's sheer heaven.'

'Sorry, but I was never mad about the Wreckers', the very name of the place puts me off. No, I shall stay at the local and nothing will change me from that. Have you seen Alan Thane recently?'

'I have indeed. He is here in the room now, would you like a word with him?'

'I'd love it,' and she handed over.

Plainly the two men were glad to hear each other and to talk. Then when they had finished, Bridget had a last word trying to persuade him to stay here in the Wreckers' House with them, for she knew that Miss Sutcliffe would not be happy otherwise, but he was adamant. 'I wonder if he believes in ghosts?' she asked herself, 'And if so how dangerous that could be!' She told Alan how glad she was that he was coming.

'He was a wonderful surgeon at hospital,' she said. 'The man who actually got me down here. I should never have heard of it if it had not been for him. I am longing to see him again.'

Alan said, 'Look here, don't you think he might be the man to help us with Julian? Does he know about him?'

'Only vaguely, I think. He certainly said nothing much to me about him.'

'If you are really worried, he is the man to confide in. I think he could help a bit.'

'Maybe you have got something there.'

She went up then to tell Miss Sutcliffe what had happened. She was very proud of her house, and the extreme comfort she had for guests.

'Mr. Dene has telephoned. He can't get here today as he has a small operation, but he will be coming along tomorrow for certain, and that is something to look forward to.'

'What a shame! And I had planned a lovely dinner for him tonight.'

'Let's have that one tomorrow instead. If he won't stay here, at least he can come to dinner.'

'He's a very obstinate man, you know.'

'You're telling me!' and she laughed.

For a few moments Gay sat there, her face twisting a little from a headache. Then she said, 'He never has stayed here, he always goes to the local. I think he has some idea (and lots of people have) that this place, having belonged to the wreckers, has a ghost or something. It hasn't. I'd be the first person to know it if there had been one here, for ghosts do that for me.'

Bridget said nothing. Then after a time she said, 'He will be sure to have his dinner here, I think.'

'Yes, quite sure. I never feel that he gets on well with Julian, they are as the poles apart.'

'Doctors are used to people who are as the poles apart,' and Bridget said it slowly, 'I should not worry.'

But she knew that her patient was thinking of something else. 'I want them to be fond of each other. I love both of them, and to me it seems all wrong if they don't get on.'

She changed the subject then and talked more about the doctor. He was a very old friend of hers, she had known him almost all his life, she supposed. She thought that he had done more for her than anybody else in the world. He had thought that Cornwall would be a better climate for her, and it had been on his advice that she had come down here in the beginning.

'I owe him a great deal,' she said gently.

Later in the day Julian appeared, and the first thing Gay told him was that Mr. Dene would not be coming today, but would definitely be over tomorrow. Instantly the whole of Julian's face changed.

Later Miss Sutcliffe said, 'It must be one of Julian's bad days, he has these at times. Nothing seems to go right for him. He does not often care for older men, I suppose that is what it is. But he never stays down in the dumps for long.'

At the same time, when he came out later on into the garden where Bridget was gathering some flowers for the household decoration, he was in much the same mood, and admitted it.

'I get the sulks,' was what he said. 'Maybe it is that I get jealous of Gay and all her friends. I am very fond of her for all she has done for me, for the great woman she is, and I owe everything to her. I always suspect doctors, which is nasty of me, and anyway Dene and Gay have been friends for years, but somehow I feel that . . . oh well, maybe I don't understand what it is that I do feel, but that is the answer. Maybe I suspect all doctors.'

Bridget felt happier gathering flowers with him. The garden here was lovely, perhaps flowers grew better here in Cornwall than anywhere else in the world. He told her that he must drive her inland to the woods where at this time of year the rhododendrons were still pink and crimson, and that pure unbelievable white of theirs. She knew she would love it.

That afternoon he did take her to see Mousehole which he said was an enchanting spot, and they just had the time. It was quite unlike anywhere else that she had ever been to, but she was beginning to find that this was the secret of this part of the world, it was quite different. The tiny streets, the artists' houses, the way you could even walk into a house and admire the pictures, and be welcomed. The comfortable little hotel with strawberries and cream for tea. He wanted to take her to visit Gulval where they made mead, near at hand. She had thought it was some fairy-tale drink, not a real one at all, but something out of another world.

'Well, it is almost of another world,' Julian admitted, 'but if we do go there we shall be late home. And you know what Gay is over things like that. She wouldn't be too pleased. We must do that on another day.'

She said, 'Of course.'

They had to race to get back in time for dinner, but they managed it. One thing was definite about Julian, though, he never tried to break any of the rules.

Gay had had a long sleep. The headache was not yet quite right, and she was disturbed lest it upset tomorrow, when she did want to be at her best to greet the doctor.

'You'll be all right,' Bridget promised her, and gave her one of her tablets last thing, to make sure.

She did not stay late with her, hoping she would get a longer night, and she came downstairs. Julian had gone out somewhere, but

Smutty started to bark, and she saw Alan approaching. He had come across when the day was done; he very often came in then for a drink, and Gay loved to see him.

He walked into the house in those long loping strides of his and came through the great hall on to the lawn where she was walking.

'I happen to know that Gay likes seeing me,' he said. 'It gets tiresome being ill. How is she?'

'Fair to middling, and I have sent her to sleep.'

She was glad to see him. He was one of those men who could give her a certain confidence, which was very comforting. She said, '*I* find the house kind.'

'Yes, it is now. It has lost its old ways. But then you happen to like Cornwall.'

'I do. Enormously. It has something which, when I go back to my hospital when Miss Sutcliffe's own nurse returns, I shall always remember and think about.'

'You'll go back?'

'That was the arrangement.'

He waited a moment, quite a long moment, then he said, 'I shall miss you.'

She said, 'That's kind of you, and I shall miss you, and everything here. Very, very much indeed.'

They walked across the lawn towards the house.

It was a very beautiful garden, which had

been most admirably laid out. A huge dark yew tree stood to one side of it, almost black against the pearl softness of the night, its great arms lifted without a sound, a silent tree. Close to it a large clump of rhododendrons was still in flower, and still glowing even though the half light was already draining them of their colour. Alan Thane was speaking of his own people, who had been born in this village and had died here, as had grandparents and great-grandparents before them. He had had an elder brother, lost overseas in the war, which had been a terrible grief to them, and which he had always held had killed his mother. The brother had joined up at merely eighteen, had gone overseas, as he had said 'just in time to march across Europe and sing the victory song'. But he had been killed within three days of landing.

He said, 'My people were part of this village, we belonged here, and will belong here until the name dies out. I believe some of the Thanes were here when fat, little Queen Anne came down this way to visit this part of the world, or so they say. Part of the house was standing then, not recognizable now for so much has been done to it since then, so many changes made.'

She said, 'How lovely to live generation after generation like this, in the same house!'

'One gets attached.'

'Of course.'

He changed the subject. 'I believe you have

161

the imagination to write a book.'

'*She* said that. I wish it were true.'

'Why don't you try one day? They say the germ lies deep within everyone, and given the chance one day it comes out. This would be your opportunity to give it a chance.'

She laughed at the idea.

'Nursing is quite an arduous job on its own,' she said. 'You'd be surprised how tired you get when the day is done, though private nursing is nothing like the wards. All those beds!' By now the night was coming up dark, and Bridget was surprised that it was so late. 'I must go,' she said.

'To bed?'

'To bed. Julian is out somewhere with the doctor. I think they do a pub crawl, or something, at this time of night.'

'Or something!' he said and laughed.

She went indoors and upstairs. The way Alan had said those two words made her suspicious, she did not know why. Once, she remembered, Sister Tutor had told her that never when one was working in private, was it wise to worry too much about the people for whom one worked, only for the patient, and his or her good. Only about the one who really needed her.

She tiptoed into the bedroom very softly indeed. The curtains were drawn back, and she could see the lights of ships at sea, tranquilly moving across the quiet waters. Gay was awake, and turned to look at her.

'I thought you'd be asleep.' A tremendous sense of guilt came into Bridget's voice. 'Alan brought you a book. It is one which he says you very much wanted to have, and it only came down today. If I had known that you were awake I should have brought it straight up to you, so that you could start it right away.'

'I have been quite happy. How kind of Alan! But then he is an intensely kind person. I wish he would marry. He would make such a sweet husband for some nice girl, and somehow I feel that his life alone is somewhat wasted.'

Bridget said nothing. She waited a moment, tidying up, that eternal tidying up which is so much part of a nurse's life; then Gay said, 'I am so enchanted that Frank Dene is coming again, he is such an old friend of mine.'

'It's odd he won't stay here in the house,' said Bridget.

'Yes, but he has always been like that. But his coming down here is the best news I have had for ages. Even if I *have* been feeling vilely ill, his coming here will make all the difference in the world for me. I know that.'

'Old friends are ever the dearest.'

'I know. I hope you have lots of old friends, my dear,' and her face warmed.

'Not so many. Mine has been rather a lonely life.'

Gay said, almost as though she were

163

confessing something which she should not have done, 'My worry is that he and Julian do not get on too well together. I wish I could do something to put it straight, but that is not easy. One day perhaps.... Both of them are dear people, but....'

Bridget said, 'You mustn't bother about it. Go to sleep for now, but remember that tomorrow is always another day with its own worries, and its own joys too.'

'You're a dear.'

Bridget put the final touches to the room, straightening the bed linen, and as she was finishing Julian came in. He came quietly, almost as if he thought the patient might be asleep, and would now wake up. But as he *had* come, there was nothing she could do.

'Stay with her whilst I go down to get her her last cup of pick-me-up,' she suggested.

'Why not let old Janet bring it up for her?'

'Because poor old Janet has got bad legs, and they are old, whilst mine are still young. Because I should hate to run her about, and there is no reason in the world why I should not fetch it for her myself.'

She went out of the room with the feeling that she had got the better of him, and knowing quite well that this delighted her. But he must not stay too long. As she went to fetch the tray, she thought what a joy it would be to see Frank Dene again tomorrow, and if only she got the chance she would ask him some more questions about this place, about her patient and about young Julian whom Gay had adopted and adored, and whom she trusted, perhaps wrongly. 'I am so glad he is coming,' she thought, for there was much in which she needed help, so many questions she wished to ask him.

Janet was at the foot of the stairs with the tea all ready. She also was worried that the doctor would be down tomorrow, for he was a man who loved his food, and she could *not* think what she could get him for what she would have called 'an extra special'.

'Tomorrow is another day, wait till it comes,' and Bridget laughed.

'Is Miss Sutcliffe tired again?'

'Yes, yes she is.'

Janet nodded. 'It's a shame she should have so much to bear, and her so good.' She stood still for a moment, and then said, 'I've known her for years, I have.' She spoke kindly. 'She is the most beautiful lady as ever was, what would do anything for anybody, but I gets worried for her.' Then she spoke more quickly, twisting a corner of her apron. 'There is lots of things going on here what isn't right. I knows what I says, and one of these days something terrible will happen, and I mean that.'

She paused, with cold horror in her eyes.

'I know what you feel, and she has been ill a

long time with this wretched thing, it is hard to see any improvement. I too know that there is something odd going on.' Sister Tutor would not have approved, but she had to say it.

'You and me's in this together, Nurse.'

She said, 'Yes,' and put out her hand. Then she took the little tray and walked slowly up the stairs with it. Suddenly as she reached the top she got the impression that at this moment she was standing on the very edge of danger. Tomorrow with Frank Dene here, surely it would be easier? Maybe things had already taken a slight turn in the right direction. Maybe it would, as her mother used to say, 'all come out in the wash'.

CHAPTER SEVEN

That night Bridget did not sleep well.

She was restless, and for no reason. When she had taken the tea to Gay last thing they had all said goodnight quite happily. The connecting bell between Gay's room and her nurse's did not ring all night long. She prayed that it meant that the patient had had a good night, and whatever else happened, the great doctor would be down here with them. He was the trusted friend of both of them, and the man to whom Bridget could tell everything.

I'm worrying myself unnecessarily, she thought, and tried to settle down to sleep, but somehow she could not go off, so that she got up earlier that morning than she would otherwise have done. She knew that there were dark rings under her eyes, and when she looked in the glass the bad night showed itself quite startlingly.

She was down to breakfast early, but Julian was already there, helping himself to fish from the silver dish on the side, and he said that she looked tired and quite ill.

'Oh, I'm right as rain. I didn't sleep too well, but that is nothing,' was what she said.

'You worry too much.'

'Born that way,' and she passed it off with a laugh.

He ate his fish with a zest, he was one of those men born with a rollicking appetite who can go on eating whatever else happens. 'Well, *don't* worry, for it never pays,' he said quite gaily. 'What is to be, will be. Everything that can be done for Gay is being done, and you ought to know that. It's no good making yourself ill because of her, you know, as it won't help her in any way.'

'I know, but she is so brilliant, and writes such enchanting books; it is such a shame.'

He was regarding her with those eyes which always gave the impression that he could see through her. 'Of course! Gay is a charmer, and the whole world knows this.' Then he looked across the table at her, and he said, 'You don't trust me, do you?'

'Don't trust you, what do you mean?'

'Just that. I feel that you don't trust me entirely, as you should.'

'But of course I do! I think you don't like my being here to take charge of the medical side, when you have been doing far too much for the patient yourself. I ... I felt you were a bit fed up with me because I would not let you give her medicines behind my back, but I *was* in charge of the nursing.'

Instantly she knew by the change of colour in his face that he was annoyed with her for saying this. For a moment she saw that he did not know what to say, then he spoke again, not angrily, Julian was far too clever a young man to lose his temper, and she ought to have known this.

He said, 'It's a bit tricky when one has always done it for the patient, and suddenly a stranger butts in. . . .'

'It was not exactly butting in, the doctor sent me here.'

'Well, you turned up, didn't you? I get jealous for Gay; it is understandable, of course, because she means everything to me, and I am suspicious of strangers.'

'A *trained* stranger,' she reminded him.

She knew at once by the change of colour again and the way he looked at her, that he resented it. 'If it comes to being trained, what about me?'

She should never have said, 'But you did not finish your training, and even I did finish mine,' but the words had slipped out before she had the good sense to silence herself.

He said nothing for a moment, just leaned across, lifting the silver lid of the fish dish, and helped himself to some more from it. Then, quite calmly, he said, 'I daresay much of what you say is true, but nobody could have been more trained in looking after Gay than I was. I did everything for her, poor lamb, and I happen to love her.'

In a quiet voice Bridget said, 'Everybody loves her, for she is a charming person, nobody could help loving her. Both of us love her,' and then impulsively, 'I wish you and I could be friends, real friends, I mean.'

He said, 'Oh, I suppose I get jealous at times. Put up with me, there's a good girl, Bridget, and let's kiss and make friends? We both love her, and that is the trouble. Any long illness drives me mad with worry, surely you appreciate that?'

She avoided the question and said, 'These injections she is having? *They* worry *me*. She is still getting them, isn't she?'

He looked her straight in the eyes. 'Yes, she is,' he said.

Perhaps when he was honest he was even more difficult to manage than at other times.

Perhaps she should never have challenged him, yet the enquiry had slipped out of her lips before she could stay it. It is not easy to be tactful when in this mood, she knew, and she really was very worried. 'I am sorry to bother you, but I must know.'

'The injections are for these sickening headaches she gets, and this particular thing is the only one that ever stays them. And it does do away with them within the hour.'

'What is it?'

'Femergin,' he said calmly.

'Does the doctor know?'

'Of course he does. How do you suppose I got the prescriptions if he didn't know?' and for one second she saw that he was again fiercely resentful.

'Please don't be annoyed. This is my job, I have to know.'

'Well, and now you do know.'

She got up from the unfinished breakfast feeling that she still wanted to talk it out; yet it was getting her nowhere and did nothing for her. As she went out of the room he reminded her that the doctor would make an early visit today, for both of them were going out fishing. She in turn reminded him that Frank Dene would be here for lunch.

'Well, how can I change my plans because he runs to a surprise visit? I don't see why I should. And anyway he is an E.N.T. man and nothing to do with poor Gay's worries.'

'They are old friends, and he will want to know all details.'

'And he won't be getting them out of me. You'll have to tell him what you know; you are the nurse.'

'But I don't know everything; until a few minutes ago I had no idea that she was having Femergin injections. Nobody had told me.'

He was darkly furious, and changed when he had one of these moods, so she walked out of the room. She had the feeling that things were coming to a head, and that perhaps when she came to think about it, it was a very good thing that Frank was coming down today. At least he could give her the benefit of his advice.

It was a busy morning.

First of all there was the usual trouble with Janet. Although she was perfectly capable of producing a first-class meal, and doing it extraordinarily well, she was inclined to get fussed when it was for anyone who she thought was a 'real gentleman' or 'somebody great', and she felt this about the big London doctor today. There had been bother with the butcher who could not send her the steak she had ordered. All gentlemen liked steak, what should she do?

Bridget did not want the patient to be worried, and made out a list, none of which seemed to satisfy Janet, who was a martinet when it came to the ordering of meals. Finally, they settled it between them, and then Bridget could go upstairs. Mercifully, it was one of the patient's better days, when she was far more herself. She was excited about meeting a dear old friend, for she was very fond of this man, and only hoped that he would come early. Bridget was not sure that he would, for he had things to finish up with the patient whom he had come all this way to see. She said he would possibly be late.

Yet he came early.

She saw a big grey car coming down the lane, and wondered if it could be his, for his cars were forever grey, and when it turned the right corner as he neared the sea, she gave a squeak of joy.

'I believe he is just coming.'

Gay was thrilled. 'You rush down and meet him,' she said. 'Give him a drink first, he always wants that first thing, and welcome him. Meanwhile, I will try to compose myself for the nicest visit of the year.'

Bridget would never forget going down those stairs three at a time, she was so thrilled. She had never been down them so fast before, and as she came to the bottom one the doorbell rang, and she saw the old butler approaching out of the back of the house. She stood there for a moment, undecided; she longed to rush at the door and fling it open, but knew that this would hurt the old man and worry him to death, and not for the world would she do that. The door opened, and the brilliant sunshine flashed in. She heard Frank's voice, such a kind happy voice, the voice of someone whom you could always trust. Other patients had said that. He was an inspiration when he just walked through the wards in hospital, what Sister Tutor had called 'a *real* doctor', and that meant just Frank Dene himself.

He saw her coming across the hall to him.

'So there you are, Bridget! How nice to see you again! And I am sure you are putting the patient back on to her feet. Well, well, well, what a day this is!'

'You had a pleasant trip here?'

'Grand. And my last patient is all the better for seeing me, also, which is to the good. Now I have come here, and this is always home to me. It looks just the same. The pleasantest entrance hall in England, and always with flowers everywhere.'

'You'd like a drink?' In the background the old butler hovered as he always did, waiting for instructions. Luckily Frank knew his own mind and drank the same thing every time, and the old man shuffled off through the dark green baize door at the far end, to fetch it.

Frank sat down on a crimson velvet sofa. 'And how are things?' he asked.

'I've got an awful lot to tell you, I'm afraid.'

'And I've got a very short time. All the hours

I spend here are stolen time, for I am supposed to be back in London operating soon. I have snatched two days. I think dear Gay deserves that much. I want to find out how she is progressing and if more cannot be done. Now, tell me everything.'

The old butler appeared again with the silver salver, and set it down beside him. Then he disappeared. He had a way of coming and going, as do all these old-time servants, so that one hardly knew that he had been.

Frank said, 'It is lovely to be back here again, Bridget, one of the most beautiful things that has ever happened to me. I say this every time, and the curious thing is that every time it is true. Dead true. This place never alters. Same old butler. Is Janet still here?'

'Of course she is!'

'She would be! And the adopted nephew?'

'He and the doctor are out fishing at the moment, but should be back later.'

'You like him?'

She should have held back what she felt, but there are moments in life when the difficulty is that one can restrain oneself no longer. She was in love with the place, with the charming house, and with the blueness of the sea which lay beyond it. She adored the kindness of her patient, the way she was for ever giving little gifts, caring for her more like a mother than a patient, but under it all there lay things that she did not understand. She knew that she was not alone in this, for dear old Janet was dubious, and the butler, although he never said a bad word against Julian, had rever said a good one, and quite plainly never would.

'Well, what is it? Obviously something is very wrong,' and Frank Dene was speaking in that quiet voice of his which they had known in hospital as the 'operating theatre voice', the voice with a ring to it.

'I don't like the fact that Julian is giving her injections about which I am not told.'

'What do you mean?'

She told him of the needle she had found in the ashtray.

'You think Julian gave it to her?'

'Yes, I do.'

'Did she say anything?'

'Not really. He tells me that the injections are for her bad headaches, and that they are Femergin. Yet she had that injection at a time when she had no bad headache, and did not need anything to ease the pain. In fact, she was in no pain then.'

'Is she worse after the injections?'

'I don't know, I have evidence only of the one injection.'

'I think I had better have a word with the young man. He isn't qualified.'

'No, he left after the first year.' She found herself laughing, and was half ashamed to be doing it. 'He and the hospital did not see eye to eye, I believe. He found the book learning a bit much; he has a poor memory and all those names sent him dizzy.'

'Did they now!' and there was a twinkle in the man's eyes. 'I can well believe that, most of us are whirling with them, but it is one of those hills one has to climb in life if one is ever to get anywhere down the other side.'

'I know.'

'If I ask him questions, he will know that you told me.'

'Yes, of course.'

'And I have *got* to find out.'

She said, 'You will find out that although he is outwardly charming, so much so that one rather believes one is cheating oneself, he is a very evasive young man. We—we may not get another time alone together, I fear, and this is something which has to be settled. I am a little afraid of going on as things are. If there was some ghastly mistake, it could be laid to my door. You do see this?'

'I hope that I am seeing everything. I want to put this straight.' He came to a stop, then he said, 'And he is her heir?'

'She has told the world that she has left him everything when she dies.'

He said, 'Shakespeare once wrote, "Lord, what fools these mortals be!" He would have done better to say "Lord, what fools these women be!" for that is what it boils down to. You don't like him?'

'No, not at all.'

'I'm glad I know. Now I will go and see Gay. She has you here, and this should be the biggest help. Look here, my dear, we have known each other for a long time, and what we are going to do together is finally to settle this wretched business. I cannot go to London until I have some good idea of what is going on here, and why. Now let's go and see her?'

Bridget rose to lead the way. She was thankful that at last this man had come here, thankful that she had told him as much as she had, and grateful that now she had someone backing her. Something was very wrong, and she could not lay her finger on it.

They went up the handsome staircase together, and down the carpeted corridor to Gay's bedroom. It was one of her good days, for which one thanked the powers that be. She held out her arms, and her delight in meeting a dear old friend was surprisingly entrancing. Bridget brought an easy chair for him beside the bed, and then left them there.

Later Gay asked for their lunch to be brought up here, so they all had it together. When the room had been built, one of the windows opened onto an exquisite balcony with a tremendous vista of the sea. On this balcony the doctor and Bridget ate their meal, against a most

177

remarkable setting, and were able to talk to Gay, still inside the room, as they ate.

Already Bridget had the feeling that help—very real help—was at hand, though none of it was going to be easy. She knew that, but for the first time since she had got here she felt able to face the future with courage. At last she had some backing which until now she had been entirely without. She was convinced that something strange was going on; she thought that the doctor knew more about it than he should have done, a man she could not trust, and never would, but this was insufficient to make her unkind about him. Now everything rested with Frank Dene.

Mentioning Julian to Gay, she said that she adored him, it was the strong abiding affection of a woman who had not had a tremendous amount of love in her world, and had possibly spent most of her love on her own books. They disclosed some side of her nature which she could not otherwise give to the world in general.

The great doctor was careful to show nothing of his own feelings. Candidly, she said that she had adopted Julian because he was all alone in the world and had no people, and she wished to be good to him, that was all it was. She cared deeply for him, he was kindness itself through her illness, and always ready with something to ease her pain. That made Frank Dene suspicious. He asked no questions which could possibly disclose what he was after, but he listened to what she had to say.

It was late afternoon when the fishermen returned together, and by the look of things it had not been one of their better days. To Bridget it always seemed that when this happened fishermen blamed others, not themselves. She thought they were fed up as they got out of the car, still in their fishing things, and looking rather untidy. They came inside for drinks as was usual, the butler saw to all that, and then Julian tore upstairs to see Gay.

'Hello, darling!' he exclaimed, 'has the unwanted guest gone? If so, three cheers for the Union Jack!'

Somehow it seemed that Gay was not too pleased with the enquiry, for she said, 'I am awfully sorry to disappoint you, but Frank is staying at the inn for a couple of nights, which is very good news for me, because I love having him down here.'

Bridget could feel that Julian was furiously angry at the very idea, for all the colour rapidly drained from his face, and she saw the sheer indignation that was curling at his lip corners. Hurriedly Gay tried to calm things down. She told Julian that Frank was dining with them tonight. She had invited Alan Thane to join them, and it would be an enchanting dinner party.

'I should think it would kill you,' said Julian,

and he went off like a bear with a sore head.

Gay said nothing at all, but Bridget knew that she was deeply disturbed that it had been taken this way. She went very quiet.

It was later that she told Bridget a secret that she had got up her sleeve. She was feeling better, so very much better, and she had a surprise for them. She intended to come down to dinner for the first time for months. It could be done quite easily, and when the dining-room doors opened and dinner was announced, there she would be sitting at the head of her own table! There was a luggage lift at the back of the house, and she could get her chair into it, and go down unseen by anybody. She was like a child with a new toy.

'This is to be the wonder evening of my life!' she said.

'I only hope I shan't get into serious trouble for letting it happen,' Bridget murmured.

'We are together in this, dear. We'll see each other through. I want to do it more than anything I have done for years, and whatever happens, even if it kills me, I'll do it.'

Naturally, Bridget had to help her. She went inside the luggage lift, and thought it possible—the butler told her it was safe. Somehow Bridget did not like it, for the luggage lift lifted up to its *métier*, it creaked and it groaned and made strange heaving sounds, which alarmed her.

It had been a considerably better day for Gay.

She was enchanted to have the doctor here with her, had had a good night, and although she had awakened with a headache this morning, it had worn off very soon.

'You should have rung the bell for me,' Bridget told her. 'I would have given you something for it.'

'Julian came in to say good-bye, he was making an early start, and he gave me something to ease the headache.'

'But why did he want to wake you up to tell you he was going off early?'

'I don't know. He hoped to get through in time to spend the rest of the day with all of us, and he gave me something to ease the headache.'

Bridget tried to hold back that feeling of intense irritation which came to her at times, but he had no right to do this, and she chafed against it.

'He ought not to do that whilst I am here. It is my job to look after you and do everything I can. I like being asked. There need never be any anxiety about waking me, or anything like that. Truly I do *not* mind,' and she hoped she said it with sincerity.

'It so happened that Julian was with me.'

'I see.'

She said no more, but tidied up for the day. Although she knew that the patient liked the little maid to do this for her, Bridget preferred to do it herself for today. Throwing away the empty bottles, wisps of cotton wool, and the innumerable rather untidy trails of illness, was something that she felt she ought to do.

One after another she had cleared them away. Even emptying the waste-paper basket piece by piece. It was an automatic part of her work, something she had been taught in a lecture on private nursing. One must, of course, never suspect one's patient, but it was within the realms of good nursing to be cautious. Carefulness pays. Waste-paper baskets should be gone through. In hospital these things could actually become automatic, they are something one does just as taking a temperature or a pulse. The waste-paper basket had the wisps of cotton wool, a label from a medicine bottle, and a small cardboard container, which she instantly suspected, for she knew what it would have held. Going back to the basket she found the tiny glass tube, with the long neck broken, and the contents gone. It *was* a hypodermic injection.

'What is this young man doing giving injections to *my* patient and telling me nothing?' she asked herself, and kept the refuse for Frank Dene to see. This had got to stop.

Femergin possibly, she thought, but suddenly became more suspicious. Anyhow, this was evidence which she could show the doctor when they talked tonight. She said and did nothing for now.

But one thing was certain, the lift at the back of the house which was reserved for luggage would take the patient down in her chair for dinner. Bridget would help them, of course, for she felt that the very nature of this special surprise would do her patient good. Even Fanny, the little maid, was intrigued by the brilliance of the idea.

'I am afraid Julian is likely to be angry with me when he sees me at dinner,' Gay warned Bridget.

'I should not worry too much. When he realizes that you were well enough to come down, I am sure he will be delighted. However long is it since you went downstairs for dinner?'

'Longer, much longer, than I care to remember.'

'You are in very good hands, for I will look after you myself and do everything I possibly can to help you. You will be the big surprise when the doors open and the guests come in. You yourself sitting again at the head of your own table! Imagine it!'

'Yes, it *will* be a thrill.'

Bridget only hoped that her patient would not overtire herself by getting *too* thrilled at the thought, for this was always possible. Gay herself was like a young girl with her enthusiasm. She was elaborately dressed, and the soft blue of the material showed what a glorious light gold her hair had once been, and how like the flax itself her eyes had laughed and shone. She was wheeled along the empty corridor to the lift at a time when everybody was getting themselves dressed and ready for dinner, and nobody knew what a great surprise was in progress. Janet was helping. Janet was only too enchanted to be of help, and she wheeled her mistress to her place at the head of the dinner table, and closed the doors behind her. The table looked exquisite. Perhaps, so Gay thought, the fact that she had not seen it for a few months meant that it seemed to dance for her and to look utterly beautiful. A long oval table with seats all round it, and a huge bowl of mauve and pink sweet peas in the centre; the silver was sparkling, the old man took the greatest pride in it; and now all she had to do was to sit still until dinner was announced, the double doors flung open by the exultant butler, and the guests entered.

Janet was delighted. All along she had felt that her unhappy mistress spent far too much time in that bedroom upstairs and some arrangement could have been made to get her downstairs, out into the garden if possible, or in a bed in the enclosed veranda if the weather was inclement. But now Gay was in a whirl. It was almost as if a new world had opened its doors for her, and she had passed through into the land which it offered.

'In some ways this is quite the most

wonderful day of all my life,' she told herself.

'This is going to surprise everybody, Nurse,' she told Bridget.

She had, at Gay's request, changed into her best new dinner dress, one of those which she had bought on that romantic outing when, for the first time in all her life, price did not matter. It was the palest blue, with something of mauve in it, as one finds in the petals of delphiniums when they stand in their noble spires in the garden. The dress swept round her, and at the breast she had pinned a spray of tiny roses. Alan had given them to her from his garden this morning, and they looked delicious. She felt exalted by the dress, which a good gown can always do. I'm glad I came here, she thought, even if Julian is being difficult, even if there is something going on under it all which I do not understand.

Bridget had asked Fanny, the little maid, to zip up her dress at the back, and she had just finished when they heard the booming sound of a bell pealing close by. Almost in the very building. It rang like a convent bell which calls the faithful to prayer. It rang strongly, dominantly, and with determination, and then it stopped.

'Whatever is that?' Bridget asked Fanny.

'It's the bell on the house.' The girl whispered as though the very thought of it alarmed her, and she could not speak aloud. She said, 'Once

185

the wreckers lived here, and they were bad men.'

'I know.'

'At sea there are buoys with bells on them, and these bells warn ships to keep away, or tell them the route to travel along.' The girl was a fisherman's daughter, and she knew these things.

'But the bell is here? On the house?'

The girl spoke again in that quiet voice. 'The wreckers placed the bell here to give ships quite the wrong idea as to where they were. Then they would come in straight on to the rocks. They lost their ships and their lives this way. It was a most dreadful thing.'

'But why does the bell ring tonight?'

'When the lady bought the house, she had the bell re-hung, and now it rings only when the wind is in a certain direction.'

'It can't ring often?'

'No. It only happens once in a while; maybe there will be six months before the wind is exactly right again.' Yet even as she said it the bell echoed again, sending that strong, strident, somewhat eerie note right through the house.

'You don't like it?'

Fanny shook her head. 'Nobody in this part of the world likes being reminded of the wreckers,' was what she said.

'I don't suppose it will do any harm really.'

Then Bridget finished dressing and went

downstairs. The others were having cocktails in the library, and she knew that her job was to hurry them and get them through into the dining-room for the great surprise. She was only too well aware that Gay would tire easily. She had not sat up to dinner downstairs for many a long day, and one must not strain her more than one could help.

'Time we went along to dinner,' she said. 'My patient wants us all to go upstairs and be with her afterwards, so let's make it a shade early, shall we?'

'Right!' That came from Frank Dene, ever ready to help.

They went across the hall to the double dining-room doors, with the old butler standing there, and he flung them wide. That was the moment when everyone was amazed. Julian was the one who showed it most, for he gasped aloud, also he dropped the half glass of sherry which he had been bringing with him from the library.

'Good lord!' he said, 'how has this ever happened, and how did she get down here?'

'She wished to do it, and to surprise you all, and there was no reason why she should not do it,' Bridget explained.

Julian had gone white with anger. He said, 'I care for her, and know what is good for her and bad for her, and what she should do or not do. She should *never* have done this.'

For a single moment it almost seemed that there was going to be a real row, for he looked so indignant, then it was Frank Dene who came forward very quietly. He had always been the best man at settling rows. He said, 'Why all this fuss?'

'Because Gay is not well enough to make this effort. Because it is far too big a strain on her,' said Julian, and his voice was bitingly angry.

'I should have thought that Nurse's training put her in the position of being the better judge.'

'I did some medicine,' Julian reminded him, and there was real fury in his voice as he spoke.

Frank smiled tolerantly. 'Not your full time, really. Nothing like your full time. You have to remember this. The change will do Gay good. She needs to come down if she can, and see more of what is going on around her. It will do her good, and now let us make this the extra special meal which she can really enjoy.'

Julian had run out of words. He still looked furious, Bridget could see this, and that was when the great surgeon turned kindly to Gay.

'I congratulate you on a very bright idea,' was what he said. 'There is no reason in the world why you should not often come down on your good days. Come down and see the world. It cannot hurt you. You need make no effort, nothing to aggravate matters, but just sufficient to be happy, and I am quite sure that personal happiness in the way you live your life will do much to make the actual disease more bearable for you.'

Janet had served a special meal. She had put her best foot forward to do this, but somehow or other it seemed that their appetites were a little lacking. Bridget could not imagine why this had happened. Julian had gone coldly silent; before dinner he had been gaily chattering, but now for some reason he was hardly saying a word. He was also playing with his food. Yet the patient herself was gay, never had she looked happier than she did now, at the head of her own table, chattering to them all.

They had finished the main course—really Janet could make the world's best entrée—and now she was getting the table cleared a little for the dessert, when Dr. Forbes arrived.

They heard the crocky sound of his car outside. It was a very ancient car, and apparently he was one of those men who are always having accidents. Janet had told Bridget this. When he was shown into the dining-room, with the strawberries and cream and the rest of the dessert on the table, he was still wearing his old workaday suit, a man who cared little how he looked, and appeared to be one of those people who feel personal appearance to be a bore. It had struck Bridget that he would feel vaguely out of it in this beautiful dining-room with everybody else well dressed, but if it did concern him he did not show it for a single moment.

He sat down with a drink, refusing the dessert, and he said that he had had a hurried supper at home. Things had been very busy at evening surgery; it was a night when people all came together, the curious thing about all surgeries being that they worked in certain ways on certain nights. He was a man who talked without showing one single expression of how he was feeling. Bridget thought to herself, if only one could tell something about him, it would be easier, but one couldn't. His face betrayed nothing.

It was Frank Dene who seemed to take control of everything. He had always been like this. At hospital he was in command of a situation, never a conformer to pattern. He said, 'It is something of a record that tonight Miss Sutcliffe is down here with us. Something of a cause for celebration, I should have said, but whatever we do, we must not overtire her.'

'I am not tired,' she said, and her voice was enchanted. Bridget could tell by the way she spoke that she was enjoying every moment of it.

'Then we will finish the fruit and the coffee, and then if she wishes it, she could be wheeled round the garden.'

'I'd adore that,' she said.

'I volunteer to do the wheeling,' Alan said.

'You shall be the one,' she promised.

Bridget glanced at the other three men. There was something almost rocklike about the doctor's face at this moment, something she could not read, something she did not understand. Julian Clare was looking angry. He possibly would have felt better if he had been the one who had planned the evening. She knew he was in a furious temper.

They finished up fairly quickly and Dr. Forbes asked Julian if he could come to his house to arrange the next day's fishing. Then Alan went to Gay Sutcliffe's chair. The sun was setting now, the west rosy.

'How lovely it looks!' Gay said.

'And the air is so sweet.'

'Yes, the air is beautiful.'

Alan wheeled her first out on to the veranda, then down on to the pergola path which ran beside the lawn. It was a radiant evening, one of the loveliest products of high summer, the sun still bright, the sky bluer than the delphiniums along the border. An evening all life could enjoy, and the fact that Gay had made the effort to come downstairs had been rewarding.

It was Frank Dene who spoke of it. 'You ought to do more. You really ought to do more like this,' he said. 'When you have a better day, why not give yourself a chance, because this *is* what you need?'

'Julian feels it is bad for me.'

A frown came over Frank's face. 'Looking

after your health is not Julian's job. He is not a doctor, and I should have thought that you would do far better by listening to your medical advisers.'

'Dr. Forbes is keen on my resting.'

'I know,' Frank said, 'but I don't think *he* knows. Wasn't he trained somewhere up north, not a London or a Scottish hospital?'

'Yes, but he is very kind.'

'He seems a bit remote,' and Frank Dene frowned. 'I think you need someone to build up your own personality, you know. To make *you* better. It has done you a world of good to come down tonight. Now don't let's overdo it; after this, back to your room before you get too tired and spoil it all, and I don't mind betting that you will have the best night's sleep you have had for a very long time.'

'At least I shall have something more to think about than the four walls of my bedroom; than the fact that I shall lie there till I die, and. . . .'

He interrupted sharply. 'You won't lie there till you die. Get that right out of your head, my dear, because it is not true,' and he said it reassuringly. 'I am determined to get you on to your feet again, and round and about. Able to write more books, and the world has need of them.'

Alan thought that the evening had been a miracle of an idea, one of those things that could not possibly do any harm, and would help Gay enormously. But then they decided that she was tiring, and it was Alan who took her back to the lift, and Bridget went upstairs with them. The party was over (her part of the party at any rate), and it was now time that she went up to bed to rest.

'I shall do it again. Don't let them prevent it, please,' she begged, 'for I think that Julian disliked the idea. He likes keeping me tucked up high and dry in bed, and to me sometimes— just sometimes—it becomes a prison.'

'And with a long sentence to serve,' said Alan. 'I tell you one thing, I am glad the old friend came down for a few days. I am sure he will help, and will produce something to make you better. There are new drugs going, you know.'

'But they never work.'

He had lifted her out of the chair and on to the bed, turned down, looking cool and lovely. 'That always happens some of the time, but never all the time,' he told her. 'Some day something will work, and then life will begin all over again.'

He went back downstairs, and when Bridget looked at her patient she saw tears in her eyes. Very gently she said, 'Those are the tears of happiness, and never worth the spilling, remember that. I believe that today we have started a new era in which you will get better, very, very much better.'

She nodded, and dried her eyes. 'I am afraid

Julian never likes Frank being here. They have never got on together.'

'Does that matter, as long as we get you better? Does anything matter but that?' and impulsively the girl kissed her patient.

She slipped her carefully into bed, for putting clothes on and off hurt poor Gay, so one took care. Then she opened the windows. She could hear the men talking in the garden, and even if the sun had set a little lower, the day was still bright and fair, and the evening air sweet.

When she had finished, she left some magazines available for her patient and for Janet who was with her, very proud of her success with the dinner, and full of joy that for the first time for weeks they had got her mistress downstairs for dinner. It was a glorious evening.

As she went down the wide stairs into that luxurious hall, with the doors open on to the beauty of the radiant summer's evening, Bridget realized that someone was standing on the front door step; she could see her through the open door. It was a woman probably in the early thirties, rather fancifully dressed, not in good clothes (the sort of clothes a woman envies), but a trifle over-smartly. The hair was pale, too pale for truth perhaps, the very white-gold hair which a woman 'touches up'. She had a pink and white skin and keen blue eyes. There was something about her which did not appeal to Bridget, and she imagined that the old butler was too busy cleaning the silver from the dinner, in the far pantries, to have heard the ring.

She herself went to the open door.

'I am so sorry. Have you been ringing long? We were all upstairs or in the garden, and a bit out of earshot. I am afraid that the butler is a shade deaf. Who was it you wished to see?'

'I did not mean to come at an awkward moment. I really wanted to see Mr. Julian Clare.'

'Oh! I am afraid he went out about half an hour ago with the doctor, they wanted to fix up a day's fishing tomorrow.'

The woman's face changed. She was maybe older than Bridget had thought at first; there was something different about her, something that she did not quite understand, she realized, and with some apprehension. It was a hard face, a stern face, although it was so pretty with that painted prettiness which can be utterly charming.

'I can leave it till tomorrow,' she said.

'He will be out fishing early, but will be back about six.'

'I will come then.'

'Is there no message you can leave me to give to him, for I *will* give it to him? Your name?'

'No matter. I shall be back.'

For a second the girl hesitated, almost as if she was reluctant to leave the step, almost as if it was upsetting that the mission on which she had come had not been fulfilled. Reluctant in one way, uncertain in another.

'Can I help any more?' Bridget asked. 'I am not the daughter of the house, or anything like that. I am looking after Miss Sutcliffe whilst her own nurse is away on holiday. Maybe I could help?'

'So you're a nurse? Well, well!' and then without saying anything, and with never a farewell of any sort, the woman turned, went down the path to the gate, and passed through it, carefully closing it behind her without even looking back.

It was absurd to have the feeling that there was something wrong here, but this was exactly what happened to Bridget. She stood staring after her visitor, and trying to place her. For half a second she wondered—quite idiotically—was Julian secretly married, and he had not dared tell? Was there at the back of his life something that he wished to keep unknown? He was a secretive sort of man. She closed the door and came inside. That was when she saw that a man was coming across the great hall to speak to her. It was Frank Dene.

'Surely not another visitor?' he asked.

'A lady friend wanting to see Julian.'

'But he went out half an hour ago to fix up some arrangements for tomorrow's fishing.'

'I told her that.'

'A lady?' The eyebrows shot up. 'But I might

have guessed just that,' and he changed the subject. 'How is the patient now that you have got her to bed?'

'Better. Tired, of course, she had to make an effort to get through the evening, but she did get through it and in no mean manner. I do agree that she should be out and about more, even if it strains her. I have the feeling that whilst she is under Julian's thumb she won't be doing it. He worries me.'

The doctor nodded. 'That young man has dangerous habits, and a brief training in medicine was no help. It could be a menace.'

How well she knew that! How thankful she was that Frank realized it, and that she had this moment in which to speak to him!

She said in a low voice, 'Ever since I found the needle I have been scared stiff of Julian. I think he is giving her something other than Femergin.'

'Does the G.P. know?'

'Julian says he does. He is a strange sort of man, one of those men whom one never sees smile, and somehow there is an atmosphere about him which really worries me. He keeps getting at me. I think he didn't like the fact that I came down here to take the place of the nurse with whom he has been used to working.'

'Were they great friends?'

'I don't know about that, but I think they got on well together.'

Frank went rather quiet, taking a long time to light one of those stubby little cigars, which he so often used. Then he said, 'Now, look here, there is far more going on in the Wreckers' House than you or I know. I realize this. I am determined to save Gay whatever I do, only I can't stay here for ever. I'll do whatever I can because I take a serious view of it all, and I believe that to save her life I have got to clear the trouble up, and right now.'

Bridget had tremendous faith in Frank Dene, for he was one of those great men, a man who left no stone unturned. She remembered being told this when she had first come to hospital. He turned to her now.

'You like being here?'

'Yes, and I adore Miss Sutcliffe.'

'I know. She is an amazing woman, and we have got to save her. Thank heaven Alan Thane is in the picture, for he is a man who can work miracles.'

'He has been a great help to me so far, and I am sure he would do anything he could, but I distrust Mr. Clare. Outwardly, he can be a charmer, but I cannot rely on him. He has a curious nature. He knows a little about medicine, which is not as it should be, but there we are.'

'Read, mark and learn,' he said, and putting out a hand he touched hers. 'We face the truth, Bridget, and by this I mean what is actually happening here. This young fellow obviously wants Gay's money, and she may live on for years. I never know quite how he got here, and what is the actual truth behind him, but I don't think it can be anything good.'

'I know nothing, and I hardly think it likely that he would tell me the truth.' She might be ashamed to put it this way, but at the same time she laughed.

'You're right.' He paused. 'Now let's go and find Alan. Don't say anything to anybody about the woman who came to see Julian.'

'But why ever not?'

He chuckled to himself. 'There is a destiny which shapes our ends, rough hew them as we may. How often have I seen that come true!'

CHAPTER EIGHT

The next day was another radiant one, for they were having a spell of heat wave which made everything enchanting. Gay Sutcliffe was no worse for the effort that she had made last night in coming down to dinner, and after that being wheeled round the garden. It seemed to be right as Frank Dene had said, that change of scene and the fresh air were the best possible things for her. She must have more. Julian had stayed sulky about it all. He disliked Gay coming out of her room, and insisted that she would pay for it later.

It was a glorious day, and because it was bright, Bridget took Smutty out with her after lunch, and went across to the farm to return some books. Miss Sutcliffe was fussy about books that she had borrowed, and the moment she finished with them she liked to get them back.

Bridget went out of the gate, Smutty bounding beside her. He was an attractive little dog, enchanted by walks, never bending his knees, just bouncing up and down as though he were mechanical. He rushed to come with her.

'Here we go, Smutty!' she said.

As she crossed the road to approach the farmhouse, she ran into Alan. He was carrying a very young lamb in his arms, the harassed ewe following him, piteously bleating as if she thought he would deprive her of her lamb. Yet all the while there was that element of faith in her clear brown eyes, the thankfulness of the sheep who trusts the shepherd, and always.

He saw Bridget. 'You ought not to have bothered to bring the books back,' he said.

'My patient gets very worried if they are left lying about, and is for ever urging me to come along with them.'

He said, 'I shan't be a moment, but I must put this wee babe into his pen, after that we'll go indoors and get some coffee. Come with me?

The ewe won't hurt you, she will never take her eyes off the lamb, he is all she wants.'

They went up the road at the side of the house by the lambing yard; here were the pens, the hurdles closely packed with yellow straw to keep out draughts. Alan went to a corner and laid the young lamb down there in the straw. Instantly, the mother went to him, nuzzling him over and over, making strangely soothing little noises of her own. The lamb bleated back as much as to say, 'I'm going to be all right.'

Bridget watched them.

'How lovely they are together, and how fond you must get of your own animals!'

'That's the hard part, for the time comes when they have to go to market, and I hate the thought every time.'

'One can care too much?'

He smiled. 'Of course! The shepherd who does not love his flock is not much of a shepherd. Look how they watch me. If I put out a hand one of them comes to me,' he held out out a hand and three ewes moved over towards him, and nuzzled him. Somehow she had never thought that they would have this much intelligence.

'Oh, they are intelligent all right but people do not take the trouble to understand them,' was what he said.

He looked so tall and strong, this big man whose whole life had been spent with animals and bringing new lambs into the world. 'They are my children,' he said, 'and I do vow that no man ever had more amusing or prettier children when they get a bit older.' Then he linked a hand in her arm. 'Come into the house? I thought last night was a most successful party, and it did Gay no end of good. I still feel that chap Julian is not the right influence for her. How do *you* feel?'

'Rather the same way.'

He said, 'God forbid that I should condemn, but there's something odd about a man appearing out of the blue to settle down with a woman old enough to be his mother, then getting her to leave everything she has to him.'

'Yes, that had also occurred to me.'

He said, 'But I mustn't criticize.' They went into the big sitting-room with rugs on a polished floor, and the huge ingle, and she could imagine that when it was necessary the very tiny lambs lay here in baskets. He poured out some coffee and brought it to her. 'Can you keep a secret?' he asked her. 'A real secret, I mean?'

'That is part of our job. Nurses have to keep secrets, and sometimes it is not easy to do while giving the impression that you are speaking the truth,' and she smiled at the idea.

He changed the subject. 'You wonder why I live here all alone, I daresay.'

She was surprised that he had hit the nail on the head. 'To tell you the truth, yes, I do. I should have thought that you would have been very much happier with a wife.'

He paused, stuffing some tobacco into the bowl of a pipe with a yellowed thumb showing that he done this before. He said, 'I did marry once. Nobody round here knows, and it was for a very short time, a few days, no more. It was fourteen years ago.'

'Tell me about it?' she suggested, for the nurse in her recognized the sudden longing to confess the truth and give away the story.

'I wasn't a very strong lad, and this in spite of divine Cornish air, the open air life, and everything which should have made me strong. I had to go to Switzerland for a time, right away into the mountains there, with a brilliant doctor in charge and marvellous air.'

'And you went?'

'Yes, I did.' She did not ask any more questions but gave him his own time, sitting quietly there drinking the coffee until he spoke again. Then he started, 'It was quite a wonderful hospital, very different from English ones and English medicine. They did everything for you and let you go your own way quite a lot of the time, which helped. Too many of them had but a short time to live, Fiona was one of them.'

'Fiona?'

'Yes. It is an unusual name, but her mother had wanted it, and the poor lady had died when her daughter was born. I suppose the father gave her that name just because of those conditions. She was alone in the world, too, young, lovely, a very sweet person. She had come with a blood disease to the clinic. Leukaemia.'

'I see.'

'They tell me that ... even now ... today ... there is no cure for it.'

'One day there will be, and they have some new methods, but for the moment we do not know enough.'

He paused, then he spoke again, hurrying it a little. 'I don't know why I should tell you about this, seeing that nobody else in the world knows of it, and certainly nobody round here. We were both patients. I got better, she did not.'

She said, 'I'm sorry,' in a low voice.

'Poor Fiona! She had had so little from that brief life of hers, so very little. I had life itself, something on which she was losing her hold. She grieved that she had never married; she was twenty, there should have been loads of time, but she did not see that. Her horror was that there was no time left. She had wanted a white wedding.' He sighed deeply. 'You know what women are about this sort of thing.'

'And then?'

'I married her. I gave her the one day to dream about. The happy memory which she would take with her for ever. We had a party and a huge cake, orange blossoms and lilies, everything that she could possibly have wanted. It was a dream to remember. She died a few days later. I don't know if you could call that being married, but I felt that it was the one good deed I did in my life, to make a dying girl's dream come true. She was happy that day, oh, so happy!'

She knew that there were tears in his eyes as he spoke, she knew that in some way he had made himself very happy, too, in spite of the fact that Fiona had died so soon after.

'I—I don't talk about it. It is one of those things over which one draws a curtain. That's all.'

After a moment, one in which Bridget was half ashamed to find her own eyes misting, she said, 'I think you did a magnificent thing, something that very few men in the world would do, and it must have given the poor girl tremendous joy.'

'I think it did.' Then, after a long pause, 'I am relying on you to tell nobody round here, for they haven't got a clue. It is the sort of thing that not everybody would understand, you know what some people are.'

'I do indeed. You might almost say most people.'

He said, 'There is one thing that worries me. It seems idiotic of me to say this, but it is about Gay Sutcliffe. I—I have always had an idea that

that chap Julian might do the same thing.'

'You don't mean marry her?'

'Well, that is exactly what I do mean. I may be maligning him, and hope this is untrue, but I feel that he would do anything to get hold of her money. That could be his idea. I hope she is not stupid enough to do something foolish like that, but she has had a very sad life with this infernal illness, and she hasn't married. Most women want to, they get the idea that they have lost a lot if they miss the boat.'

'I should not have thought she was like that. Only the other day she was speaking of the idiocy of a girlfriend marrying a man who was twenty years her junior.'

'Was she now!' and he went silent.

She waited a moment, then she said, 'You think she might do it?'

'I think this young fellow is fairly attractive to women. He is not the sort who intrigues a man, with those gay manners and good looks, but I should have said that he could travel a long way with a woman, and that worries me.'

'But she would *never* marry him!' The thought was horrifying to her. 'I don't imagine the thought has even crossed her mind.'

'I hope not, but it has been haunting me for quite a long time.'

'Only because you are full of a deep sympathy. I always doubt if Julian has this same abundant sympathy for Miss Sutcliffe as he puts on. I would think it highly likely that he has not. It would be a dreadful thing indeed if this did happen.'

'But it could happen.'

Bridget was quite petrified with fright.

For no reason at all, one of those strangely absurd things that people do, acting on a sudden impulse, she said, 'Last night a woman came to see him.'

'A woman?'

'Yes. She wouldn't give a name. I thought she was a little odd, but then I was born with a suspicious nature which may cover a multitude of sins.'

'Is she returning?'

'She said so.'

'That might be the best thing in the world, if he is going to have girl visitors to the Wreckers' House; then I imagine that poor Gay will get sick of the whole thing and anything could happen. She might be the answer and able to change everything. Was she young?'

One hates beng rude about other women. Bridget had known that the woman was thirty at least, possibly more, and that she had lived life. She had guessed that a story lay behind her, a long story perhaps, who knew?

'She wasn't very young.'

He nodded. 'Well, the future has its own secrets to guard; one never knows.' Then briskly changing the subject, 'I do so hope you persuade your patient to come down for a meal again. It is high time she got better, and I feel that Julian keeps on rubbing in that she is ill, and makes her pander to it.'

'*I* don't make her pander.'

'I should never have thought that you would,' he said.

He walked to the gate with her. They glanced into the lambing yard to see the little lamb again, standing up on the weakest legs ever known, waving slightly to right and left, and saying 'Baa-a' in the most plaintive little voice. 'What a sweeting!' she thought. Then she returned to the Wreckers' House.

She had no doubt that in spite of the effort which yesterday had entailed for her, Gay was in far better form than she would have anticipated for her.

'Getting up does you good,' she said.

'I shall be doing whole lots more of it,' she snapped back. 'I had a bit of a headache early on, and felt slightly below par, but Julian was wonderful.'

'Julian should not give you medicines, I am here for that. You ought to remember that Julian is not a doctor.'

For a single moment a cloud passed over Gay's brow. It was that little passing cloud, and Bridget dared say no more. She must keep quiet.

The dressing-room was a small room,

beautifully fitted with cupboards round the walls in pale shell pink, the colour of the lining of those spotted shells which at certain times of the year are washed up on the beaches. The carpet was the same colour, and the dressing table of walnut stood in the window. It had not yet been tidied this morning; usually it was done before now. There were things lying about, even the paper basket was not emptied. She saw a wad of cotton wool lying beside it, and she had not used any cotton wool herself this morning. She would never know why she reached down and picked up the little wad; as she did so, something slipped through her fingers, on to the basket itself, and as it touched the hard wood it gave a tinkling sound, like a note of music.

She reached after it.

When she retrieved it, she found it was a broken ampoule, the end cut off, and the contents gone. No more.

'This is always happening here,' she told herself. 'It *must* be Julian who is giving Gay these injections. What are they, and why is he doing it? I don't believe they are Femergin.' She picked up the decapitated ampoule and wrapped a piece of cotton wool round it, pushing it into her handbag. At that moment she did not know why she did it, save that she wanted proof of what was going on in this house. Something *was* going on, she was sure of it. What did she do next?

It was one of those mornings when everything seemed to be curiously unnatural. That ampoule in the piece of cotton wool, and she still had it in her handbag. It was a tiresome day, everything going wrong, nothing working to pattern, and in the afternoon Janet called her. 'That lady's come back again,' she said.

She came quietly into the hall and saw that the young woman was sitting there on one of the heavy red velvet chairs. She had picked up one of the glossy magazines and was turning over the pages.

Bridget tried to remain calm as she had done before. 'Good afternoon,' she said. 'I am afraid Mr. Clare is still out fishing, as I told you yesterday he would be.' She smiled encouragingly, then added, 'As I said, he ought to be back by six, or so I should have thought. He is not usually later than that.'

She got the idea that the girl was summing her up. For a moment she said nothing, then she began again. 'I do want to see him, but when he hears who I am, he won't be wanting to see *me*!' She gave a dry little laugh, one of those laughs which in hospital they had nicknamed 'whisky laughs'.

'If you liked to come back again about six o'clock, he would be almost certain to be back.'

'Why should I keep running all round the country for him, I should like to know?' and she sounded angry.

'I'm very sorry, but you see, I can't help it, can I? And I did tell you.'

The woman looked at her. It was a pretty face, but a very hard one. The dyed fair hair was beautifully done, one had to admit it, the dress an elaborate one and well worn, but she had hard blue eyes and there was something about her mouth which was cutting and cruel.

'I suppose I go away again and come back. Only next time I shall dam' well wait.'

'Yes.' Somehow Bridget could say no more; she did not know quite what to say. 'Shall I give him a name when he comes in?'

'You can tell him it's Veronica.'

'Just Veronica? No other name?'

'That is all. It will mean a lot to him, as you'll find out, and whatever happens I shall be back.'

She rose, shook down her skirt, and walked across to the door. Bridget went with her. She had the uncomfortable feeling that surely there was something that she ought to do or say at this particular moment, but there was absolutely nothing that she could think of.

As they reached the door they saw Alan Thane. He was standing there with a great bunch of the most exquisite white roses in his hand, which suddenly Bridget remembered that he had promised Miss Sutcliffe last night. He saw there was a visitor.

'I am so sorry. I've come at an awkward moment, I'm afraid, but I promised these last night and thought I must bring them round.'

'Not at all.' Bridget spoke quickly. 'The lady came to see Julian, but he is out fishing with the doctor. I have told her that he should be back by six. May I introduce you? See, I ... I don't know your name. This is Alan Thane, who farms all the land round here; and you are. . . ?'

The woman looked at them with a strange glint in her eyes. 'I'm Mrs. Julian Clare,' she said, and walked away.

CHAPTER NINE

It was completely shattering, and the absurd thing was that neither of them flickered an eyelash, nor did anything. The woman walked down the drive and made straight for the far gate, without so much as a glance over her shoulder. She had gone before they even seemed to wake up to the truth.

'You don't suppose for a moment that that's true, do you?' Alan asked.

'She seems a most strange person. When she came here yesterday she seemed very angry that Julian was out. Now she has been back again this afternoon. She seemed to be angry, offhand, and not one bit helpful; she said that she had come to see him, and he would *not* be pleased to see *her*. She has the most

212

objectionable manner,' but somehow Bridget thought the final parry had been made as a joke.

They entered the great hall together. At this time the sun poured into it and lit it with a light that was almost fairytale. They sat down side by side on one of the long high-backed velvet seats.

'What do we do?' Bridget asked.

'I think the first thing to do is to ask Julian himself what this is all about. I suspect he has a story to tell. What about Frank Dene? He is coming over today?'

'Yes.'

'Right! Tell him exactly what has happened and ask for help. He dislikes Julian, of course, most people do. I feel that if he had been married he would have mentioned it, in case she took the law into her hands and turned up here.'

'Save that in life people usually overlook the big dangers, and because of it go further into deep water,' she said. 'I am most concerned as to the effect it will have on my patient. We must not let her suffer.'

She had not bargained for Janet arriving on the scene, and joining in. She had, she said, seen this young lady in the village once or twice during the last week and would very much like to know what she was doing here, for privately she did not think as how she was that much good.

'It's nothing to do with us,' Bridget told her.

'No, but I feel she brings no good with her,

and I get worried for Miss Sutcliffe.'

'Don't worry.' Bridget tried to soothe her down. 'Let me take her tea up to her, please, she ought to wake now.'

'You—you won't tell her nothing about that young lady?'

'I won't tell her a single thing that will *hurt* her, that I do promise you.'

She went upstairs with the tray, which according to Janet's laws was entirely wrong. When she entered the bedroom she saw that Gay had awakened and was sitting up in bed, looking refreshed and better.

'My tea, and to the minute!' was what she said. 'How good of you to bring it up for me! I dreamt that we had a visitor here.'

'You dreamt correctly. A girl did come round, I spoke to her myself. She was not wanting to see any of us, she wanted to see Mr. Clare, and he is out fishing.'

Gay looked at her.

'I have a funny habit of getting very exact dreams,' she said. 'That was what I thought myself. A pretty girl who came to see Julian, but what I did dream also was that life was never quite the same afterwards.'

'But how silly that was! How could a strange girl coming here change things like that?'

'I don't know.' She sat up in bed and with a twisted hand tried to help herself to a small iced cake. 'Has she gone?'

'Yes. She is coming back later. She does not want to see any of us. I don't think we matter a hoot to her. She is looking for Julian, and I told her he would not be home again until about six o'clock.'

Somehow this seemed to relieve Gay.

'Is everybody coming to dinner, and if so is there another good dinner for them?' asked Gay after a moment.

Bridget laughed.

'You don't trust poor old Janet very far, and she is so good, too. She will have got everything nicely settled, I know. I did have a word with her. Don't worry.'

She started to tidy up the room again, part of her job when the patient woke. This and that out of place, and she saw cigarette ash in the small ashtray beside Gay's bed.

'Have you been smoking?'

'Smoking? No, of course not! Julian had a cigarette when he came to say good-bye before he went off fishing.'

'I . . . I did not know he had been in.'

She laughed at that. 'Oh yes, he is a dear boy, never leaves me without a good-bye, bless his heart.'

Bridget picked up the ashtray, and took it into the adjoining dressing-room. At this moment she was inspired by something which seemed to be outside herself, beyond herself. She emptied the ash into the washbasin, and there was a lot of it, and as she emptied it she heard a faint warning chink. Instantly, she knew. Her hand went down to the used hypodermic needle. 'Not another one?' she asked herself, and now she knew that she was on to something that was dangerous. Something was going on about which even though she had suspected it, she had had no true knowledge.

She picked it up; it was an old needle, bent as the previous one had been, and she slipped it into an envelope. 'This goes straight to Frank Dene,' she muttered.

'You're a long time, Nurse!' It was Gay calling to her.

'I'm sorry. I was tidying up, there is always more to do than one expects, you know. Much more.'

She came back into the bedroom.

'I couldn't come down again tonight, you don't think? Another big surprise?' her patient asked her.

'No, not tonight,' she replied, and then, 'The doctor wants to have a long talk. I think you will need a rest, but we will all come up here and be with you afterwards. You need not worry that you will be alone, because that shall not happen.'

She finished the tidying-up, and fetched the flowers which Alan had brought with him; instantly they occupied her attention.

'This,' Bridget told herself, 'is going to be a

momentous evening.'

★   ★   ★

Frank Dene arrived. Alan was with the dog on the lawn, and this was her chance.

She said, 'There was another needle in the ashtray today.'

'Another one?'

'Yes, it is in this envelope. And an ampoule from the waste-paper basket.'

He took them and put them into his pocket, then he said, 'Something very dangerous *is* going on here, Bridget, and it has got to be stopped now. She has left everything to this young man, and he knows it. It worries me.' He paused, then he said, 'Tonight is going to be the showdown. Whatever happens we have got to be careful that Gay does not get a severe shock.'

'Yes.'

'The injection was not Femergin?'

'*I* have given no injection today, so I have no idea what it could have been. Julian must have given it, when he went in to say good-bye to her before he went off fishing.'

'Yes. You have no inspiration about it?'

'None,' and then she added quickly, 'But I have a vague feeling of something being desperately wrong. Of evil being very near to us, and it terrifies me. I . . . I *am* terrified.'

'Of course, but you need not be. This girl

arriving has possibly been the solution to it all. I'm glad this has happened, it may be the way out. All along I have felt that this young man is no good, and I have been suspicious. It is extremely hard to bring things actually to a man's door, and the arrival of this young woman could be the answer.'

'You—you won't go back to London yet?' Bridget asked him.

'Most certainly not! I want to see her through this. I have *got* to see her through it. What is more, I am dining here tonight. I feel it is the night when I shall be wanted here.'

They heard the sound of a car in the drive, which probably meant that the local doctor and Julian were arriving back. Almost instantly there was the barking of Smutty showing his reception, and then their voices as they came into the great hall together. It had not been a good day, it had been one of those wretched ones when what they had caught had been only worth putting back into the sea.

'There are moments in life when fishing makes you sick,' said Julian. He flung off his jacket. He looked very handsome standing there in a light shirt and the close-fitting trousers. He was one of those men who always wore his clothes remarkably well, and looked his best in them.

'You mean you've got nothing?' It was Alan who asked him, coming into the great hall through the french windows.

'Now for some tea?' Bridget suggested.

'Something stronger and more comforting than that,' said Julian. 'Besides, it's getting late for tea,' and he turned to the doctor. 'What about your evening surgery?'

'They'll be there in their hordes. They always *are* there in their hordes, just sitting around waiting for me. One quick drink, and I must be going.'

It was Bridget who poured it out for him, and watched him gulping it down. She wondered how much this man knew. He was a man whom she actively disliked, a most undesirable feeling to have about any other fellow mortal, but she *had it*. He would not have another. He put down the glass and bolted for it. Now there were the other men and herself left together.

It was Frank Dene who spoke.

He said, 'Things have been happening a bit here, Julian.'

'What things?' and then impulsively, 'Don't tell me that Gay is worse?'

'Gay has had a very good day. Possibly the injection she had this morning was a help. Who knows?' and he said it in an ice-cold voice which somehow Bridget knew could cut.

'Did she have an injection?'

'She did.' Frank paused. 'Nurse brought me the used needle.'

'But Nurse must have used it!' At the same

time his colour had changed. He was a very unfortunate man in that he had never been able to command the colour that came and went so rapidly in his face. 'I know nothing about it.'

He said no more and there was silence. Somehow it seemed to be a strained silence, with four people, all deeply concerned in it, sitting there looking at one another.

'Who do you suppose gave the patient this injection?' Frank Dene asked.

'I haven't a clue.' Now he was in a wild burst of indignation. Bridget did not think that she had ever seen him quite so flamingly angry as he was at this particular moment. 'You would imagine that I was poisoning her by the way everybody is behaving. Gay is the best friend I have ever had. If she died, I should lose everything. I tell you that I could not bear to live if anything happened to her.'

Icily coldly, Frank said, 'But you would of course have sufficient to live on, wouldn't you?'

Again came the silence. It lasted longer than it had done previously, and then Julian spoke again. 'You are insulting me. I have done a tremendous lot for her, more than anybody else in the world, and she would tell you so. If she died, it *would* break my heart.'

Coldly, the doctor went on speaking. 'You did some medical training, and presumably you know that hearts do not break as easily as all that,' was what he said.

That was when there came the sound of a bell ringing, the front door bell. The butler was slow in going to it; he was getting very old, as Bridget was always telling herself, and the door was wide open with the glowing lovely evening pouring into the house. Whoever had rung the bell did not wait for a reply. They heard her coming. She crossed the outside hall and came through the double doors into the main hall itself, the girl who had been here twice previously, the girl whose name was Veronica.

Julian had gone to the side to pour himself another whisky and water. He turned from the sideboard just as she entered the room. He dropped the full glass from his hand, but apparently did not even notice that he had done this, for it fell crashing to the ground whilst he stood stone still, then he said to himself, 'My God!'

It was Alan who had automatically risen as the girl entered; it was Frank Dene who remained sitting.

The girl spoke.

'I thought you would be surprised to see me,' was what she said. 'It's a small world, you know.'

Julian did the last thing that Bridget might have expected him to do. He rushed past them, and out through the hall to the drive beyond where he had left his car. She heard the door slam as he jumped into it, and then the whirr of

221

the engine, and the car itself shooting off.

'Where on earth is he going?' she asked herself.

It was Frank Dene who spoke. 'What on earth is all this?' he asked.

The girl explained.

'My name is Veronica Clare, and I married Julian in New Zealand when he was on the rocks there. He deserted me. I came back here to England, and have been following him. He thought he had got rid of me. He thought he could clear off and leave me to fend for myself, but I found out where he was.'

After a long moment the doctor said, 'I see.' Then he said, 'Are you going to wait for him?'

She shook her head. 'He won't come back,' she said, and she spoke almost as if she believed this to be completely true.

'If you are married you have the right to follow him but he would want to stay on here, he is a great friend of Miss Sutcliffe.'

'Yes, I know.' She said it casually, as though it was all matterless to her, and did not even concern her. 'He is bleeding her, I gather. He lives that way.' She said it as though she were speaking of a man being a lawyer, or a doctor, or a clergyman, pursuing a praiseworthy career; poor Gay was just a means of income to him.

'But he *must* return.' It was Alan who spoke.

That was when Bridget rose. Sooner or later, with the vague manner in which these things worked, news of what was happening down here would percolate upstairs to Gay Sutcliffe, and at all costs she must stop this until things had explained themselves a little.

'I must go to my patient,' she said.

'Yes, that is a good idea, Nurse,' it was the doctor who spoke.

She left the three of them talking, and all the time she was wondering where on earth Julian could have gone, and what he would be doing at this moment. He could not clear off into the blue with nothing save the clothes in which he stood up, and the car which had been Miss Sutcliffe's latest gift to him, surely? There must be something more; what could it be?

Upstairs not a word had penetrated. The one great mercy was that this was not one of those occasions when dear Gay Sutcliffe used that curious form of second sight of hers, which did so much for her.

'You've been a long time,' she said.

'Nobody was about, and I did not know what to do,' she lied casually. 'I thought I would come back up here and see if there was anything I could do for you.'

'You're a dear girl, a very very dear girl.'

She sat down beside the bed, and wished that her own heart was not making such a tremendous noise. Whatever happened she must not let her patient get suspicious. What would she do if she fainted? And in an emergency she had done this twice before in her life. The first time was at an astounding heart operation, when she had literally seen the patient's heart brought out of her body and kept working on a machine, and had felt herself swimming. Then she had said 'Oh' and had dropped. The other time had been in the post mortem room. She was never happy over post mortems, although she knew that nothing could hurt a dead body.

To faint now, would give everything away.

'Have they returned from fishing yet?' Gay asked.

'Yes, I think they had rather a bad time, for just now the fish are not biting at all well. Everyone is complaining about the catches, so Alan says.'

'He knows this sea well enough. I imagine there are none this side of Land's End who knows the coast better than Alan, with all his Cornish forebears.'

'But he has never seen the mermaid of Zennor!' said Bridget, thankful that her voice sounded so ordinary.

'Has anybody?' Gay asked. Then she said, 'The other day I got an idea for a new book to write. I had waited for an idea to come, and here it was. About a newcomer coming here to this place to live, and then disclosing that she knew a great deal about Cornwall and its people, and not all of it could have been gleaned from books.

Gradually, very slowly of course, it transpired that it was the mermaid herself, come back to atone, to live her last life on this planet, out here at Zennor again. It might be quite an interesting book to read, it would be lovely to write.'

'You write it,' Bridget suggested.

'You'd inspire me to do anything!' and then, a trifle restlessly, 'Where are the others? It isn't like Julian to come home and not run up here to say hello. Even if he has not caught a single thing, I should have thought that he would have come up here.'

'Shall I go down to see what is happening?'

'I wish you would.' For the first time those bright eyes of Gay Sutcliffe's had become anxious. She had this sometimes unhappy gift of sixth sense, of another sight, of greater understanding, so one felt, and this made one worry for her.

Bridget went downstairs. She felt stronger. The first tendency to faint had left her, and she prayed that it would not return, for she knew that her strength would be needed. She went into the hall. Alan and Frank Dene were sitting there talking. The girl had gone. She wondered what they had done with her, yet did not ask. She was the sort of person who could look after herself, and *would* see after herself, to her own advantage without a doubt.

She said, 'My patient is getting a little bit restless. She wants to see Mr. Clare.'

It was Frank who rose.

'I'll have to tell her some time. I think it will come better from me, and we can't keep it hidden much longer.'

'Would you like me to come with you, or would you rather go alone?' Bridget asked.

'I think I will go alone. We are very old friends indeed, and what she will need most at this time is old friendship. One can't expect her to know the sort of man he was, for she has formed such an entirely wrong idea of him. I'll go now.'

They watched him go slowly up the shallow stairs, taking his time, and both of them felt sorry for him. Then it was Alan who spoke.

'Come and sit down by me. This has been one of the most difficult days of all my life, and it hasn't ended yet.'

'What has happened?'

'Julian apparently shot up the lane and straight into the main road at the top without so much as a thought. It is the busy time of the day with people coming home from working in Truro, and that sort of thing. He was killed instantly.'

'How awful!'

Alan paused, then he said, 'It could have been a great deal more awful if he had lived, I am sure. I was always suspicious of him, of which I was ashamed for a time, but this is just me. I admit that I do take likes and dislikes too quickly. This is an old Cornish custom,' and he smiled.

'It is going to be shocking for her.'

'Yes. Whatever happens, do stay with her until her own nurse comes back from her trip safe and sound again.'

'Of course, but that was the contract.'

'She is very fond of you, and it is not everybody who wins her confidence, for she is reserved in many ways. You have won it, and she badly needs you.'

'As long as she needs me, and Matron will let me, then I will stay down here,' and her voice was resolute and quite determined. 'I cannot promise more, but she is a dear person and I want to do everything I possibly can for her.'

'And you like our Cornwall?' He asked it tenderly, speaking of the county almost as a man would speak of a small child whom he loved dearly, and wanted to help.

'Indeed I do. I think it is quite wonderful, and you ought to be able to see that I love it.'

He smiled for a moment, then he changed the subject. 'When all this is a thing of the past, and you return to hospital, it will be to join the staff, so I imagine, and work yourself up to become a sister. You are the sort of girl who in time would become a matron.'

She shook her head, for she had never wanted that. 'I very much hope not,' she said.

'Or you will marry for love, and live happily

ever after,' and again he smiled.

She talked casually of life, and what it meant to her. She had never thought that she would marry, and she said so. She had had the one love affair, and had suffered badly for it, because she had fallen too much in love. She drew the curtain over it now as something which lay behind her, and which time would ease in its sharpness; something that she would learn to forget, for there are things in life which have the power to hurt far too much. Now she did find that she felt better, because a new present dimmed the old past, and that was satisfactory.

He said, 'I was very glad you came down here, to help Gay Sutcliffe, for she needs help very much. It was high time that someone like yourself did something for her. I've never been too keen on that young man, Julian Clare, and am ashamed to say—very much ashamed—that this is the way that I have always felt about him.'

'I did not care for him either,' she said, 'and I felt from the first that Miss Sutcliffe would have seen through him if only she had not had such a lot of pain to bear. That minimizes one's powers of resistance.'

He agreed. For a moment he was silent, fiddling with his fingers, something that he always did when worried, then he spoke again. 'You are a very kind girl, and I knew this the first time that I saw you, travelling down this way. I was so very glad when I knew you were

coming here to be with her. Don't ... please
don't leave her before the time, because this has
happened.'

'Of course not! She needs me more now than
she did before. It would be cruel to leave her,'
and Bridget's eyes were big with dismay at the
thought of such a thing.

He lifted her hand to his lips, kissing it.
There was something about the action which
impelled her; a new eagerness seemed to rise
within her, an exuberance which she thought
that she had never felt before, and a flood of
ecstasy.

She said, 'You too have been so very kind all
along, guiding me as you did, for I was very
much a stranger in a strange land, and Cornwall
is a very strange land to me. Thank you for all
you have done.'

'I shall always be here as long as you want
me,' he said.

They were there side by side on the sofa. She
had the peculiar feeling that she stood on the
edge of a precipice, as though the whole world
trembled beneath her feet. She could not be sure
if the moment lasted for hours or was merely
passing. He put an arm around her. She could
smell the faintly sweet 'farmish' scent of his
hacking jacket, of moon daisies and ripe sorrel, a
scent which is entirely of the country. She
would never know how long the time lasted,
only that somehow she had stepped out of this

world into one a long way off.

A little while later she spoke again.

'I think I knew when we were travelling down here that you were one of the kindest men I had ever met,' was what she said.

'And now all this has happened.'

'There will be an inquest?'

'Yes, there will have to be an inquest.'

'And the girl? Where is she now? I . . . I don't like to think of her being all alone, when something as dreadful as this has happened. Where is she, for somebody ought to go to her?'

'She is staying at the pub. They are looking after her, and the doctor will visit her.'

'But she might need a woman to be with her.'

He said gently, 'You are very sweet and right, but the landlady is a dear kind soul and will do everything she can. Meanwhile, there is the district nurse.'

She said, 'What do we do?'

'Just for the moment your duty lies here with Gay. She was deeply attached to this young man, why nobody will ever know, save that affection works in a mysterious manner and these things do happen. I think you ought to go to her now.'

'Of course.'

She went upstairs into Gay's room. Gay herself was in a drugged sleep, and she knew that Frank Dene had done everything that he could for her. It was unlikely that she would

230

wake for some long time, and in that sleep would lose much of the sharpness of today, much of the pain, which would merge into something else.

She spoke to Frank in the ante-room.

'She'll be all right?' she asked.

'For her, this is the best thing that ever happened, I am sure. I did not trust that young man two yards, and the police tell me that they were closing in on him. He was wanted for a particularly unpleasant case in the south of France.'

'Not there as well?'

'Very much there as well. I think he lived on his wits, brought off a good deal, then disappeared to pastures new, and started the ball rolling again. I have had time to look up his record at hospital. It was not quite as easy as he said. He did not leave because he got sick of swotting or found the exams. too hard. There had been a great deal of unpleasantness in the Warden's house with things missing. There was not sufficient evidence to prove what one felt, though sufficient to make it seem fairly obvious, but he was allowed to take himself elsewhere, which he did.'

'You mean kicked out?'

'Just that.'

'And nobody knew?'

Frank Dene smiled to himself. He said, 'No hospital is too fond of washing its dirty linen in public, you know. They just prefer to let the trouble pass if they can, and that was what happened.'

'Now he is dead.'

'Yes.'

She asked, 'Does Gay know?'

'Not yet. We have got to be very careful what we do and say. We have got to approach it very gently.'

'It might be better if she didn't know.'

'Save that with an inquest coming on, she has got to know,' he said, rather sadly.

'Time will help us,' she said.

Time did help them in that Gay remained unconscious far longer than anyone would have expected.

The inquest, which caused unending stir in the village, went through. There could be little argument about it, the evidence was straightforward, and everyone wondered that a great deal more harm had not been done. It would have been so easy for several people to have been killed. It was over, and in fact it was the day of the funeral when Gay came round.

To Bridget's joy it all came slowly.

At first Gay just knew that she was in bed in her own room, and that someone she knew and trusted was with her. She asked no questions, which was a mercy, but dozed most of the day. In the evening, when she felt better, she asked for Julian and was told that he was not well and could not come to see her. He had had an accident in his car.

She was so accustomed to his having car accidents that she almost accepted this news in her stride.

'Not badly hurt?' she half whispered.

'Not badly hurt,' Bridget whispered back.

It was next day, when her mind was clearer, that she remembered the fact that Julian was ill, and asked where he was. When told 'in hospital', she pressed for details, and it was then that Bridget sent for Frank Dene. He was the man who must tell her, he was the man who must help her in this emergency, and going out of the room she left them quietly together. They were old friends, but there is some bad news that even the oldest friend cannot properly explain.

She went on with her work about the house, for work was the best way to occupy herself, she knew. She saw a pile of books waiting to be returned to the farm, and took them across the field herself, because she thought they were better out of the way, and Smutty knew what they were waiting for and would not let her be.

It was another of those radiant days with the sun high, the smell of flowers everywhere, and the beauty of summer at every corner. She had meant to lay the pile of books on the hall chair, just inside the door, when she got there, but as she moved to the step, she saw Alan coming towards her.

'Good to see you!' he said.

'I brought the books back.' She stood there for a moment uncertainly. So much seemed to have happened in the last few days, or was it hours? (for the moment she was actually confused by time itself). 'I thought you might be wanting them for somebody else. I know how good you are with local invalids.'

'Come along in.'

'I can't be too long. Just now I like to be with Miss Sutcliffe as much as possible.'

'How is she?'

'Marvellous. Far more so than one would think possible. I wonder at moments was she ... was she just getting slightly worried about Julian? Yet she had done everything he asked of her, she was more than anxious to please him, but I have the feeling that deep down within her there was the feeling that ... that ... things were difficult.'

Alan brought a silver cigarette box across to her and held it out to her. She took a cigarette. It was unusual for her to smoke, often she refused it point-blank, but today she needed it.

He said, 'The idea had struck me also.'

'You noticed it?'

'I wondered how anyone as clever as she is, could be deceived by someone as obvious as he was, but the sexes accept charm differently. Women are frequently attracted by the wrong

234

sort of man, men by the wrong sort of girl. I
have seen a beautifully brought-up son of the
house fall for the commonest little bit you ever
saw, and marry her, to regret it for ever. These
things happen. Gay is past her first youth, and
this feeling would not last so long with her. It
has struck me in the last fortnight, perhaps since
you came down here, and I don't know why I
associate it with that, that she was possibly
cooling off. I did hope so.'

'And now . . . poor fellow. . . .'

He hesitated for a moment, then in a very
quiet voice he said, 'People always put it that
way; I wonder why. Life comes, and it goes.
Love is a transient emotion. That is perhaps its
greatest fault.'

For a moment Bridget thought of that. Had
Gay been cooling off the man she had adopted as
a nephew? Had she somehow or other seen
through him and realized that he was not the
charmer he would make her believe him to be?
Had the accident been a blessed way out?

'What do you suppose his wife will do?' she
asked.

He shrugged his shoulders.

'As you know, she has already gone off and
back to London. As you realized at the inquest,
he was her third husband, two divorces, and
now this. She is the sort of charmingly attractive
girl who appeals to a certain type of man, and
who always wants to—and does—get married. I

235

imagine she will go back to some other man friend whom she has got up her sleeve, and for the time being they will live happily together.'

'Only that sort of marriage has no long run. It cannot be lasting.'

His cigarette had gone out, and now very thoughtfully he re-lit it. 'It won't be. Perhaps there is no certainty for her kind of woman. It is a hateful thing for me to say, but I do not mean it unkindly. She will for ever fall on her feet, for that sort of girl always does.'

'But what about the approaching time when she gets older? Too old to remain attractive to men, and that seems to be her sole career. What then?'

'Perhaps like the old soldiers who never die, she'll simply fade away,' and he smiled.

She thought for a moment, then said, 'If that is so, it is a sad thing. A woman with no future, save penury. No people. No real love, and possibly life without love at all is even worse than life without money.'

'You've got something there,' he said.

She heard the clock striking, and had not realized that the time had gone so fast. 'I must get back to my patient, she may be wanting me,' she said, and then, 'No, don't come with me. I shall run most of the way and be quite all right. I don't suppose the piskies will get me!' then, from the actual doorway and still smiling, 'I'm getting that much Cornish, you see, and after quite a short time. I half believe in the piskies, and what they can do to me.'

He nodded. 'May the piskies guard you!' he said. 'They are kind little people, and somehow I have a feeling that they will do their best.'

But she had turned, and had slipped out of the house, scared that Gay would be wanting her, and she was already late.

CHAPTER TEN

Before Frank Dene returned to London, Bridget had a private word with him. He was satisfied about the patient's progress, but he felt that she needed close attention for another three weeks at least. By then it would be near the time when her own nurse returned, and then could take over control. He did not see how Bridget could leave Gay until the other nurse came back.

He was concerned about the doctor here. He had not liked the fact that he and Julian had been such friends, yet there was little he could do about it. He had gone into the matter of the discarded needles and ampoule and had had an analysis made, finding out exactly what he had suspected them to contain. This product would have no immediate effect, nor would it assert itself to anyone watching her, but given over a length of time it would produce a gradual deterioration, and a sinking of strength.

'I had suspected something of this nature,' he said when he and Bridget were discussing it before he left.

'You surely never thought this could be going on here, in this very house?'

'I am afraid there are times in a man's life when he suspects almost anything,' he said very slowly. 'Gay has a lot of money to leave behind her when she goes, and that can be the very brick with which the cat is drowned, for it is tied about her neck. It is an awful thought, one which does not bear thinking about, but there you are!'

'It's horrifying, and to think that I got mixed up in it all!'

Frank said, 'I am sure that having you here with her has helped her very much. I imagine they all thought you would be safe, forgetting that you had me behind you, and I am not easily shaken. All that you can do now is watch her day by day, and get her well again. I believe she stands every chance now that wretched fellow has gone. Whilst her will was signed, sealed and delivered in his favour, I felt that she stood in awful peril, and she did.'

The girl said nothing.

She would be sorry to see Frank Dene return to hospital, but there was no outward and visible fear left here with her in the Wreckers' House now. She went to the gate to wave good-bye to him, and with tears in her eyes. He had been such a help, and all through her training in hospital he had been the power behind the whole hospital; she knew that she could trust him.

Even Gay saw her tears.

'Why are you crying?' she asked Bridget when she tidied the bed.

'I'm so sorry the doctor has gone. He has always been so kind to me, I miss him already, the place isn't the same without him.'

'But you don't hate this house?'

'Oh no, no, of course not. I love Cornwall, and everything it holds out to one. It has changed me.'

Gay smiled at her. She said slowly, 'One of these days you must come down here to live. You could get lots of good jobs going out nursing, if that was what you wanted, and in your spare time you would find it the loveliest place in which to live.'

'I know I should. I adore it, but. . . .' She hesitated a moment, then began again. 'Perhaps when a man or a girl starts life in a big career, they look ahead to greater things *in* that career. I should not want my future to end here.'

Gay smiled again. 'Sometimes,' she said, 'new influences come into our world, and change us. For some of us Fate points out the way and we divert our course to follow it.' Then she changed the subject. 'I have always felt that there was something compelling about this house, something which was inescapable. Fate shows the way, and leads all of us in turn. I feel within me that something more is going to happen here, because Fate is the compass in all our lives.'

At the end of a few days Bridget felt better and her patient was remarkably restored; she had not had one really bad attack in that time, which was surprising, and she came downstairs twice, a new departure for her, and one she pursued, having once done it.

Nearer the time for Bridget's departure, there came a letter from Matron's office. She was a woman who forgot nothing. She was now wondering if Bridget would be returning to her old hospital on the date she had given Matron when they had had their interview. To Bridget that date had been engraved on her heart, though she had said nothing about it to anyone else. Matron had to make arrangements ahead, of course, Nurse would understand, and as the time was rapidly approaching, she would be grateful if Bridget could give her some idea of what her plans were for the time ahead.

The girl knew that she was nearing the parting of the ways. The dreadful part was that she was not quite sure of her own mind. Ever since she had started training, she had seen the hospital as the be-all and end-all of her whole life. Privately she had thought of staying on to become one of the Sisters-in-Charge. These were the women whose valuable lives had made the hospital what it was, and to whom the establishment owed its very existence.

When the trainees were girls together, they had discussed the older women, and had dismissed them as a bevy of 'proper old cats'; now, of course, she saw them in a new light. What miracles they could work, and how good they had made the name of the hospital! There must be hundreds (if not thousands) of men and women in the world who owed everything to these noble women who had worked so hard for them.

Now she saw them as the props behind the life of the hospital, the women whose virtues one could not dispute. 'I won't be one of them,' she told herself.

She rather wished that she had not come to stay in a part of England which was entirely new to her. It was so entirely different from anything that she had ever known before, and it had had the power to change her, to influence her. Land's End for instance, so mighty at sundown, and there were moments, she had been told, when as you turned away from the sea and perhaps looked back over your shoulder for a single second, you saw there a mirage on the horizon. It was the mirage of a sun-baked desert, of glittering fascinating castles, and of palm trees. 'One day I too will see it' she told herself.

She thought of the pastureland, and of the strange superstitions of these people. The fishermen working with their boats, and the farmers with their cattle. She had seen one violent sea, just the once, since she had come here on this visit, and that had been lashing and angry. The house smelt of salty spray, one could not shut out the smell of it for days. It was a wild world when it became angry, and yet in the happy sunshine it was the last refuge of the 'little people'. Strangely enough, since she had come here to live she shared with Cornish men and women their faith in the little people, in the 'ghoulies and ghosties', and the wishes that were granted.

Maybe Cornwall is changing me, she thought.

It could be possible.

All the same, she could not delay for too long, and of course she would have to write to Matron. That was the night when she and Smutty went out walking in the wild countryside before turning in. The sun had set, and there had gone with it many of the illusions which lingered about this part of the world. She went to the moorland, had thought of going up to the piskie well, then changed her mind, and came back by Alan's farm. The lights were on downstairs, the curtains not drawn, few ever made use of their curtains. The outside world could watch if it so wished, it did not worry them. The hall door was wide open, and she saw Alan coming out of it.

'I was just taking Smutty back,' she said.

'What about a few roses to take with you?'

She said, 'Lovely! The very sweet-smelling ones if you can spare them, please?'

He picked the flowers carefully, peeling off the red thorns, and throwing them away. He prided himself that no flower that he had ever plucked, stung or hurt a friend. He brought them to her at the gate.

She said, 'It's a lovely night.'

'You brought good weather with you, you should stay for ever, and bring it again and again, we could do with it.' And then, 'The summer visitors have no idea what the autumn storms are like here. The lifeboat is out day and night. Watching her, I feel that I have seen her sink a thousand times, it is unbelievable.'

'I . . . I'd get alarmed.'

He said quietly in that soft sentimental tone of his, 'I think that you would not hate it really. They do such a magnificent job of work.'

'I know.'

He paused. 'Soon you are leaving us, and going back to the hospital?'

'Yes. My time is up, and the regular nurse is coming back.'

'Once you go, you'll never return,' and his voice was sad.

'But I have planned a holiday here, and I

243

promise you I shall come back.'

He paused, then he said very sympathetically, 'You may not realize that I shall miss you terribly. It has been delightful to have someone more or less of my own generation to talk to. I have been so absorbed in the farm, and the work it offers me, that maybe I have wasted time. I knew the first moment I saw you in the train travelling here together, that you ... that you were *the* woman.'

She tried to think of something to say, but somehow the words would not come. She stood there helplessly, her hands clasped before her. Then all she could say was an apology. 'I ... I am so sorry.'

In a low voice he asked, 'I suppose I could not persuade you to stay? With me, I mean, and for ever?'

His voice had gone very quiet; she could not believe that she had heard aright. She tried to speak, but again the words would not come. He was the one who went on talking.

He said, 'I knew even then that I loved you, in the train. That I would give my whole life into your keeping, and know that I could live happily ever after.'

His voice died away.

He put both his arms about her, and she did not offer any resistance to him, for all she wanted was to feel him close to her.

In a tender voice he told her of the future.

'You will live in this house for the rest of your life, and I will guard you and help you, and do everything that a man can to make a woman happy. I felt all this for you in the train when we were alone together. Perhaps I knew then that the meeting with you was for me the great beginning of everything that mattered to me. Perhaps I knew then that this was the beginning, the *great* beginning. Cornwall is our world, my darling, and I want to take your hand and lead you forward into its joyousness for ever.'

For a moment she went silent, then she whispered in a voice that she could not recognize as being her own, 'So much has happened that I am utterly bewildered. I ... I don't know what to say, but we are perhaps going forward hand in hand into our own world.'

He put his arms more closely about her.

'This is your home, darling, and you shall be its mistress. I am here to guard you and to guide you, to love you for ever, and that is what I mean to do.'

He laid his mouth on hers and kissed her.

She heard the sound of the sea in the distance beating against the shore; it was one of those calm nights when the waves whispered sweet nothings as they caressed the rocks, and did not speak of storms. The stars were in their myriad thousands in the sky above them, glittering on a cloak of dark purple.

Then, in a sudden paroxysm of joy, she saw all the fields as being part of her own land, her heritage in this part of the world. Green hills and valleys, the ruins of countless tin mines, and the hill tops with their groups of fir trees and maybe some wishing well, some place of fairy assignation, somewhere where the dreams come true. Suddenly she knew that this was her world, and that he was her man. Green hills and valleys, she told herself, all her own world, the world to which she had come, and where she would stay for ever.

She put both her arms about him. 'Oh, Alan, I am so happy, so very very happy,' was what she said.

Photoset, printed and bound in Great Britain by REDWOOD BURN LIMITED, Trowbridge, Wiltshire

9